Z. RAPTOR

STEVE COLE

RED FOX

Z. RAPTOR

A RED FOX BOOK 978 1 862 30778 0

First published in Great Britain by Red Fox,
an imprint of Random House Children's Books
A Random House Group Company

This edition published 2011

3 5 7 9 10 8 6 4

The Random House Group Limited supports the Forest Stewardship Council (FSC),
the leading international forest certification organization. All our titles that are printed
on Greenpeace-approved FSC-certified paper carry the FSC logo. Our paper
procurement policy can be found at www.rbooks.co.uk/environment.

Mixed Sources
Product group from well-managed
forests and other controlled sources
www.fsc.org Cert no. TT-COC-2139
© 1996 Forest Stewardship Council

Set in Bembo

Red Fox Books are published by Random House Children's Books,
61–63 Uxbridge Road, London W5 5SA

www.**kids**at**randomhouse**.co.uk
www.**rbooks**.co.uk

Addresses for companies within The Random House Group Limited can be found at:
www.randomhouse.co.uk/offices.htm

THE RANDOM HOUSE GROUP Limited Reg. No. 954009

A CIP catalogue record for this book is available from the British Library.

Printed and bound in Great Britain by CPI Bookmarque, Croydon, CR0 4TD

For James Thornton

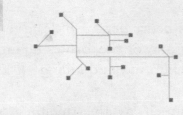

0: The Hunting

After a night spent searching the black cracks of memory, the creature was certain now. *I have a name. I am not like the others, I have a name.*

The wind ruffled the tough, ragged feathers that half-covered the creature's hide. As dawn picked at the darkness, he stayed staring out from a grassy cliff top over the ancient spite and wildness of the ocean. The sea hurled itself relentlessly at the rocks, hissing and frothing as it was thrown back, gathering itself again to strike.

The creature understood the strike of the sea, the way it battered furiously at its boundaries. *The name*, he thought. *What is my name?*

A rustle – a stamp from the forest behind him. Something was coming. Not one of the humans; the tread was too heavy. He turned and peered into the windblown darkness, scanning for unnatural movement. His snout twitched at traces of reptilian scent. His sensitive ears caught the clack of heavy claws and the sweep of a thick tail through foliage.

The creature's heart beat a little faster. He was being stalked by one of the Brutes again. All they cared about was hunting and killing.

My name . . .

He tensed himself as the stealthy foot-treads drew nearer . . . nearer . . .

In a sudden rush of movement the Brute broke cover and pounded over the open grassland, a roar building in its thick, scaly throat as it spat a stream of yellow liquid.

Nimbly, the creature threw himself forward, dodging all but the last burning drops. Hide stinging from the acid, he hit the ground and twisted under the Brute's belly, raking two sets of long, deadly claws through the unprotected flesh. Blood pumped from the wounds in a grisly shower. The Brute bellowed its pain, turned and raised a huge, clawed foot, ready to stamp down on the creature's ribcage.

But the creature was too swift. He extended his sickle-shaped claws and jammed them up through the sole of the Brute's foot before scrambling clear. With a savage scream, the Brute lashed out with its heavy, barbed tail and struck him in the jaws. He was stunned for a moment, but then coiled his own tail around the Brute's good ankle and tugged hard. Losing its balance, the Brute was forced to fall back with all its weight on its ruined foot. The agonized howl as it collapsed to the ground was deafening.

Panting for breath and tasting his own blood, the creature watched his wounded enemy squirm on the ground, pure hatred in its stare. The Brute wouldn't stop now until one of them was dead. *Why? Why did you come for me when other prey is so much easier?*

Because you know I am different.

The creature flinched as another stream of acid jetted from the Brute's hanging jaws. Spatters fell across his legs, burning, enraging. A red haze fell over his eyes and he darted forward, grabbed the injured foot, twisted hard. This was the only way to end the conflict. The Brute convulsed with pain and clawed at the grass and earth around it, heaving itself closer to the cliff edge in its struggles to be free. The creature clung on through a rain of bone-jarring blows and kicks that tore blood and quill feathers from his side.

'See?' the creature hissed. 'Should've . . . left . . . me . . . alone . . .' But as he spoke, with a sudden jolt, he let his grip on his victim go slack. The words had sparked a connection, a clue, plucked from the blood-red crevices of his brain – it was *that* he needed to hold on to now.

Less than a metre from the precipice, the Brute broke free at last. Slavering, it tried to roll clear but was too close to the edge. Panic flared in its cold eyes as with a last despairing roar it fell from sight, plunging to its death on the distant rocks far below.

Alone again. Panting hard, the creature sank to the ground. He smeared his wounds in mud to slow the bleeding, the stir of the ocean soothing him now.

The last stars faded from the sky. He felt stronger, staring across the bay to where a stone building stood in semi-ruin, hiding so many secrets. He had been trapped there for so long. Alone.

Alone. Allow . . . He could see black capital letters in his mind, hear ghostly voices. *Low. No. Kneel low . . . Lone . . .*

LONER.

'That's what I am,' the creature whispered. 'Loner.'

I don't belong here, he thought. *I cannot stay. And all those who did this to me will pay.*

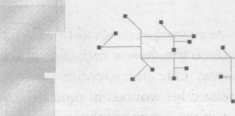

1: Danger City

Someone's following me.

Adam Adlar quickened his step. He couldn't shift
the feeling. Fighting his way through the Christmas
crowds along Fifth Avenue, he told himself to chill
for the hundredth time. *Of course someone's following
me. There's got to be a gazillion people on this street.*

It was close to 6.00 p.m., and with only ten days
to go until Christmas, New York City was heaving.
Wide-eyed tourists soaked up the sights; weary
office workers pushed past in huddles, hurrying
home.

In hindsight, Adam supposed the evening rush
hour was probably not the best time to head downtown to meet his dad. But he wasn't about to pass
up on the one time his father had actually suggested
a meal out together. Normally Bill Adlar was so
into his computer work he didn't get back to the
hotel until late, so Adam was seizing the invitation
for pizza with both freezing-cold hands. It was a
long walk, and he supposed no self-respecting New

Yorker would dream of making the journey from Midtown to Greenwich Village on foot. But Adam had ninety minutes to kill, and couldn't face the even greater crush of the subway or figuring out which bus to take.

Besides, walking had its advantages. He could hit the 'R' Zone inside the giant Toys R Us on his way – 500 square metres of the latest electronic games and DVDs. Dad had left him money for a taxi, but Adam figured if he put the cash towards a new game for his DSi it would be a much better investment.

He tried to lose himself in the cold, Christmassy moment. The scale of everything here made him feel like a tiny kid playing in the land of a giant. Tower blocks and skyscrapers rose up all around like sheer cliffs disguised with glass and metal. A jigsaw piece of night hung high above, impossibly black. Holiday lights strung about the trees and gaudy displays in store windows tugged at the eye. Steam drifting up through subway vents mingled with the smoke from hot-dog carts and the charred aroma of roasting chestnuts. Even the heavy traffic seemed festive tonight – the big cars bumper to bumper in a parody of paper-chains, fairy lights reflecting off windows and bodywork, the honk of horns sounding more like greetings than rebukes.

But Adam's feeling of being watched persisted,

and the nagging voice inside wouldn't shut up. *Someone knows what happened over the summer,* it said. *They know about Geneflow Solutions – what went down in New Mexico and Edinburgh. There might even be a Geneflow base here in New York.*

They know about the dinosaurs.

When he stopped to think about it all, it still scared him stupid. Geneflow was a secret scientific group with huge resources and even larger ambitions. Somehow they had forced the evolution of a *Tyrannosaurus rex* to the ultimate level – *Zenithsaurus rex* – known to its creators as Z. rex. Four months ago, they'd kidnapped Adam's dad, used his programming skills and pioneering video-game technology to warp the mind of their dinosaur, to turn it into a living weapon to be unleashed on any target they chose. But that 'Think-Send' gaming tech had been developed using Adam's own thought control, and he'd found himself taken too – by the Z. rex itself . . .

Adam loosened his scarf about his neck; it was starting to feel like a noose against the flesh. Sure, in the nightmare struggles that followed he and his dad had eventually broken free and Geneflow had suffered a major setback to whatever plans it was hatching. But the hidden heads of that organization were still active. Still plotting . . .

What if they're after you again, to use against Dad?

What if they're waiting till you get downtown where it's quieter and . . .

He was doing a good job of spooking himself. But then, it wasn't as though his imagination had nothing to go on. He knew first-hand the stark terror and helplessness of being alone and trapped a million miles from the everyday world. He never, never wanted to go through that again.

He ducked into a clothing store that wasn't so crowded. The guys' section was on the ground floor, so he positioned himself behind a mannequin and kept a careful eye on the entrance, watching for anyone suspicious. He jumped as a woman passed him, saw the tartan scarf draped around the collar of her winter coat and felt a homesick pang for his native Scotland.

The irony was that coming to New York had been supposed to make him feel safer. He'd struggled through a term at school, doing his best to adjust to normality again after the horrors and wonders he'd lived through. But it was hard. Especially when his dad accepted a short-term contract with a Manhattan research firm, leaving Adam to crash at friends' houses till he returned.

He had no choice, Adam reminded himself. To stay sharp, cutting edge video-game architects needed to operate at the forefront of new technology. And his dad had explained that Mindcorp's pet project was pushing at the boundaries of modern science in all kinds of ways.

At first he'd only stayed away during the week and flown back for weekends; but the commute was a killer. So for the last few weeks of his contract, Mr Adlar had taken Adam out of school and moved him into his hotel suite on West 54th Street, just a few blocks from Central Park. The park was Adam's favourite place, with rocks and rivers and meadows and hills. But always he saw the tops of the skyscrapers, looming over the trees, guardians of the city's bustle, determined to keep this green space in its place. And after several long days spent alone, Adam was beginning to feel a prisoner of the city himself. He was feeling lonely, vulnerable and . . .

Paranoid, he decided, having studied the sidewalk traffic for several minutes and seen nothing suspicious. *You're imagining the whole thing. Just get yourself over to Dad's office and drag him out to the restaurant.*

'Somewhere warm, with pepperoni pizza and a stack of garlic bread.' Adam smiled. 'Sounds good to me, and it'll taste even better.'

He strode purposefully towards the exit. As he did, he thought he glimpsed a gaunt man in a dark coat with a grey cap step back into a shop front. Annoyed with himself for reading menace into everything, Adam pressed on with the dodge and dance through the thronging crowds.

At least Midtown was hard to get lost in, a gigantic grid that was sensibly numbered and divided into east and west. Adam had studied his guide map long and hard in his hotel room so he wouldn't need to bring one out on the street and advertise to everyone that he didn't belong here. He turned right onto West 46th Street, hoping for some brief respite from the thicker crowds of tourists. He wasn't far from the neon cacophony of Times Square, with its glowing electric hoardings and acres of animated signage. To Adam, it was one of the coolest places on Earth, a million miles away from the stately, soot-blackened sandstone of Edinburgh.

As he reached the crosswalk over Sixth Avenue, again he caught movement from the corner of his eye. There was the gaunt man in the dark coat and the grey cap, leaning into the driver's window of a silver Lexus parked at the side of the road.

It means nothing, Adam told himself. *It means . . .*

Slowly, the man in the cap turned his chiselled features straight at Adam and pointed him out to the driver. Headlights flicked on, dazzling bright, as the car started towards him.

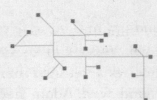

2: Chase Manhattan

Oh no. Adam felt his guts lock. He turned away, kept his gaze dead ahead as he ran across the road. *Sometimes, people are paranoid with good reason.* Struggling to think clearly he stayed on West 46th Street because the traffic could only flow east – the Lexus at least couldn't follow him. But that still left the other guy on foot . . .

Why didn't I spend Dad's money and let the hotel call me a cab? What do I do now? As his heart began to pound, half-formed ideas began to snap through Adam's mind. *Find a cop. Put on a lost little boy act and say you need a ride home.* But he knew that home in New York meant an empty room in an impersonal hotel. Anyone could get to him there. No, he needed to reach his dad. A taxi.

Doing his best to dodge people, he ran down Seventh Avenue and found himself in Times Square. Strange, alien light bathed the world from house-sized plasma screens and floodlit hoardings. The sidewalks were insanely crowded, a slowly flowing river of people, and yet he'd never felt so alone. He saw tons of cabs, but none for hire. Across the sea of people there was a huge police dispatch area. Would anyone really be crazy enough to try anything here?

But Geneflow had turned the police against him once before. Turned him into a fugitive. He realized how easily he could be snatched in this neon-soaked scrum. Whose word would the police take, anyway? *'The boy's overtired, officer, we're taking him home . . .'*

Adam felt panic rising inside him. He stepped off the sidewalk and into the blare of the rush-hour traffic where Seventh Avenue met Broadway, looking frantically all around. A gridlock was fast forming; even if he could find a cab he wouldn't make much of a getaway travelling at five miles per hour. He scanned the crowds. *No sign of Grey Cap.* But what if there *were* other watchers, walking towards him? Or right next to him already?

Desperate to put some space and traffic between him and any pursuers, Adam again broke into a run, apologizing under his breath as he pushed and half-collided with an endless stream of indignant shoppers. He picked up speed, turned right onto West 40th Street, his cheeks burning and his breath beginning to rasp in his throat.

Then he saw the Lexus, making a right turn at the far end of the street, coming towards him.

Adam turned frantically to a young couple

walking along behind him. 'Help me,' he panted. 'Please, someone is after me . . .'

But the couple just hurried past, acting as though he wasn't there.

'Please!' he shouted after them. The Lexus was getting closer. Adam darted across the street and fled through a litter-strewn side alley. It ended abruptly in a high chain-link fence, beyond which was a small private lot full of Christmas trees for sale. Looking back Adam saw the nose of the Lexus pressing into sight from one direction as Grey Cap ran into the alley from the other.

Adam threw himself at the fence. It rattled and bucked as he scaled it, his feet slipping, the wire links biting into his hands. He wanted to scream – *this can't be happening to me again* – as he heard a car door open and slam behind him.

'Adam Adlar!' His name was thrown down the alley in a low American accent. 'Wait. We need to talk with you.'

'Stay away!' Adam yelled back as he swung himself over the top of the fence. He hung on precariously for a few moments. Then the echo of footfalls running hard and close pushed him over the edge like a physical force. He dropped down into a ragged pile of broken tree branches and foliage. The needled branches scratched and bit but though Adam still fell hard, his ankles held out. The

Christmas-tree vendor, a short, stocky guy, jumped up from his chair and started shouting. 'Hey! What d'you think you're doing?'

'Stop him!' Grey Cap shouted. 'He hit my wife and stole my billfold!'

'I never!' Adam stumbled towards the tree vendor. 'Please. These guys are after me—'

'And they'll get you too, you thieving punk.' The man lunged at him, doughy fingers splayed, clutching for his coat. Frantic now, Adam dodged aside and sprinted for the exit to the lot. 'Thief!' The vendor yelled after him. 'Someone stop that kid!'

No heroes stepped forward from the small crowd gathering to gawp nearby, but Adam knew he couldn't hope for help from a cop now. As he burst out onto West 39th street he pelted onwards, bypassing the heaving sidewalk for the side of the road, ignoring the blaring horns and shouts from cyclists. Adam was oblivious to anything but the need to get away. He hit Seventh Avenue, and realized in his confusion he'd headed east, doubling back on himself. *Just keep going.* Blocks became a blur. Crowded yellow cabs, neon menorahs, police-car lights and store displays spun in Adam's sight as he forced himself to run on and on . . .

He came to Penn Station and stopped running, doubled over, catching his breath. It was like a vision – the place was heaving with cabs, picking up passengers for the rail service as fast as they could drop them off.

Hope surged through him. He ran out onto the crosswalk, although the red light glared, slipped through a moving maze of bumpers and bonnets and blaring horns to reach the station entrance where the taxis gathered. 'I need a cab,' he snapped, pressing his face against the driver's side window. But the taxi just pulled away, almost knocking Adam back out into the road. He turned to the next cab in line as it trundled forward to fill the space and collect the next huddled group of travellers. 'Please,' he said to its driver, ignoring the angry babble from the people who'd been waiting. 'I'm sorry to cut in . . .'

Then, with a sudden squeal of brakes, another taxi jerked to a halt close by, double parking. 'Hey!' A man with black, unkempt hair leaned out and smiled at Adam. 'Need a ride?'

The first cabbie stared in outrage. 'The line starts at the back, dope.'

The man's voice hardened. 'But this kid's *not* in line, is he? Sooner I take him off your hands the better, right?'

A barrage of horns went off, but Adam barely noticed the filthy looks hurled his way as he threw open the passenger door and slid onto the back seat. 'Thank you,' he panted, shaking. 'You saved my life.'

'Then you'd better give a good tip,' quipped his driver, through the thick glass partition. There was an oriental look about his features, and maybe a Texan drawl to his accent. 'You look beat, man. Where are you headed?'

Adam searched his jumbled mind for the address his father had given him that morning. 'Uh . . . can you drop me at the corner of Bleecker and Jones? I've got to meet my dad, as quickly as possible.'

'I just came that way.' The driver clicked his tongue. 'Trust me, you don't want to go to the Village.' He smiled into the rear-view mirror. 'Not when we've got your dad over on the East Side.'

Adam felt fingers of ice run down his spine. 'No,' he breathed. 'No, no, no . . .' He yanked hard on the door handle but the safety locks were on. Then he noticed that the windows were tinted so no one could see inside. He hammered at them, tried to tug them down so he could shout for help, but they wouldn't budge. Wildly, he twisted round in his seat to try the rear windshield.

Through it he saw Grey Cap and two other men in the Lexus, following them steadily through the thickening traffic.

3: Calling Out

'Who are you?' Adam demanded, trying to keep the tremor from his voice. 'What do you want?'

'We only want to talk.' The driver opened up a small wallet and slapped it against the glass partition. 'If you'd taken a cab from your hotel – which would've been *my* cab, of course – none of this would've been necessary.'

With a shock, Adam saw that the wallet showed an ID card that could barely contain its bold, blue capitals: FBI. 'Special Agent John Chen,' he read underneath. 'So . . . you and the man with the grey cap, you're the good guys?'

'Depends what TV shows you watch,' Chen said wryly. 'The Federal Bureau of Investigation has several investigative priorities, including to protect and defend the United States from terrorist threats and high-technology crimes. We believe you and your dad can help us with our inquiries into the organization Geneflow Solutions.'

Adam felt a surge of hope. 'You know about Geneflow?'

'Not nearly enough.'

'And so that's why you're after me and my dad . . . ?' Adam wanted more than anything to believe Chen, but found his rush of relief was quickly dammed. 'Why didn't you just call us at the hotel, ask us over? Why go to all this trouble?'

Chen's voice betrayed weariness as he turned onto 42nd Street. 'This is no ordinary investigation, Adam.'

'Where are you holding my dad? FBI headquarters or something?'

'It's kind of a long drive to Washington DC, don't you think?' Chen shook his head. 'I told you, East Side – he's been taken to the United Nations Plaza. There's this UN watchdog group involved now, see? They've requested this interrogation takes place on neutral, international territory.' He sighed. 'It's not the way I'd have liked this to play out, but we've all got to live with it, you know? Because you see, Adam, this goes beyond just American national security. It concerns the whole world.'

Tell me something I don't know, thought Adam.

The rest of the journey passed in silence.

Adam supposed the United Nations headquarters was unusual for Manhattan – it was a huge, glass skyscraper standing in its own space, free of rivals. Floodlights emphasized its stark form. A curving stretch of flagpoles stood on the plaza outside. Adam watched the flags as they gusted in the breeze, bright in the winter darkness.

Chen's bogus cab pulled up into a semi-circular drive on First Avenue opposite 46th Street, while the Lexus continued on its way.

'They're not coming?' Adam wondered.

'Doug and the guys have got other stuff to do,' Chen said simply.

Armed police stepped forward to meet the cab. Chen got out and showed his pass, and Adam was relieved when the officers nodded and spoke into their radios. Chen opened the rear door and Adam held his breath as he climbed out, the sight of so many guns making him uneasy. Then Chen steered him away through a gate in the wall ahead of them that led into a plain lobby. Two police escorts summoned an elevator and showed Adam and Chen inside. The doors slid shut behind them.

'I want to see my dad,' said Adam, his voice sounding thin and quiet.

'We've set up in a conference room in the basement,' Chen told him. 'Quiet. Private. Off the record.'

The elevator opened to reveal two more impassive guards, who guided them down the corridor to an ordinary, nondescript door. Chen knocked. Adam felt nerves tearing through his insides as the door slowly opened . . .

The room was long and painted cream, with a large projection screen on the far wall. A worn wooden table all but filled the space. And sitting on the nearside, rumpled as ever, was Bill Adlar – grey eyes wide through his glasses, his thinning hair mussed and adrift. 'Ad, thank God you're all right!'

'I knew you'd find a way to get out of pizza tonight,' Adam joked weakly, grabbing his father in a hug. 'Dad, I was so scared. This friend of his chased me through the city, tried to make out I'd robbed someone so he could catch me . . .'

Mr Adlar frowned at Chen. 'He did what?'

'Apologies for the cloak and dagger stuff tonight, guys,' Chen said. 'But we don't know if Geneflow Solutions are watching you already – and if they are, we don't want them knowing we're in contact with you.' He looked at Adam. 'That's why we couldn't just wait for you to turn up at your dad's offices and grab you there.'

Adam felt a familiar tingle of nerves. 'Then . . . your friends in the Lexus were trailing us to see if anyone else was following?'

'That's right.' Chen looked at Mr Adlar. 'You've got a sharp kid there.'

'I wouldn't be here now without him,' Adam's dad said simply. 'But I'd sooner we were both somewhere else. I tried to warn the FBI months ago about Geneflow and their illegal genetic experiments in New Mexico. No one seemed interested then.'

'Yeah, well, things change.' Chen looked troubled. 'Let's not forget, Bill, you contacted the FBI anonymously. And you left out some of the more, shall we say, *surprising* aspects of your ordeal.'

'I didn't know who I could trust.' Mr Adlar didn't break off his stare. 'I still don't.'

'None of us know that, Mr Adlar,' came a lofty, English voice. The conference room door swung open and a white-haired, owlish man, half-buried beneath a long, dark coat and a white, winding scarf, bustled inside. He sat down stiffly at the head of the table and shivered as though he still felt the cold. 'I am Doctor Jeremy Marrs,' he announced, 'chairman of the International Science and Ethics Association.'

Mr Adlar looked coldly between Marrs and Chen. 'Was it ethical to chase my son across Manhattan, scaring him half to death?'

Unruffled, Marrs put on a pair of gold-rimmed glasses. 'I'm sorry if Mr Chen's methods lacked a little finesse. But we required the presence of both you and your son at this meeting without delay, and the young are resilient, I am informed.' He smiled at Adam. 'I'm confident your fine young man will bounce back.'

Patronizing idiot, thought Adam. But the man's earlier words were playing on his memory. 'Science and Ethics Association? I'm sure I've heard that name before . . .'

'Whenever new breakthroughs in genetic experiments are made, the United Nations consults the Association – a loose collection of experts worldwide who consider the ethics of the work and advise on whether it should be allowed to continue.' Marrs turned to Adam's dad. 'Until recently, one of our key members in the private sector was a bio-medicine research executive called Jeff Hayden. I believe you know him?'

Hayden. Blood-soaked memories tore through Adam's head at the mention of the name. *The psycho maniac who started this whole nightmare.*

'I knew Hayden,' said Mr Adlar coldly. 'Past tense. He's dead.'

'According to his board of directors, Hayden's taken a six-month leave of absence from work,' Chen informed him. 'Off fossil-hunting some place.'

'And he sent me a video-message confirming his resignation from the Science and Ethics Association,' Marrs added, 'citing ill-health as the reason.'

Adam looked at his dad, baffled. 'But we *know* he's dead.'

'The people at Geneflow are incredibly well-prepared.' Mr Adlar leaned forward in his seat. 'If you were sent a video, Doctor Marrs, Hayden must've filmed it some time before as a contingency – to stop the authorities looking too hard if anything happened to him.'

'Possibly,' said Marrs briskly. 'In any case, I received an anonymous letter some months ago informing me of Hayden's involvement with a global network of scientific activists, working on this Z. rex project. Am I right in thinking you wrote that letter, Mr Adlar?'

Mr Adlar hesitated, then nodded. 'I didn't sign it because I didn't want to get Adam caught up in some big covert investigation. He's been through enough. We both have.' He studied them, anger simmering in his eyes. 'And it goes on. You've scared us both witless tonight. Why?'

Chen cleared his throat. 'Perhaps you should play the *other* video-message you got, huh, Doc?'

Marrs looked at Adam. 'I'm not sure it's fit viewing for the boy – even if you do consider him an expert witness.'

Adam frowned, and Mr Adlar opened his mouth to say something, but Chen was already clicking on a palm-sized remote. 'Ten days ago the doc here received an email,' the agent told them, as the projector screen on the far wall glowed with bands of colour; Adam saw an open laptop connected with an untidy loop of cable. 'The video you're about to see was attached.'

Marrs nodded gravely. 'Special Agent Chen had already interviewed me regarding the activities of Geneflow and Jeff Hayden. So when I received this video, I brought it to his attention. You'll see why.'

Abruptly, sound and colour cut in to the projected image. Adam felt his blood run to ice as grainy, unfocused footage of two creatures hazed into view. They seemed part-bird and part-beast, with dark, scaly bodies sprouting stiff quills around the shoulders. Their S-shaped necks flexed like serpents with long, fearsome jaws. Then the scene cut to a blurry image of a man running on a beach, dressed in jeans and a torn shirt, looking over his shoulder. A second later, a giant brown blur of speed and scales raced up behind him. A spray of red erupted from the man's body as he fell. Almost in the same instant, two more of the nightmarish creatures pounded into view, their heads hunched forward on thick, sinuous necks, ready to tear into their share of the kill.

Horrified but unable to look away, Adam saw the image cut to something else — a blur of red scales and bloodied plumage, something standing too close to the camera.

'Tell them.' The voice was unearthly, cold as stone. 'Tell them what Geneflow does. The danger.'

And the camera lurched to the left. The image of a woman, blonde and haggard, her dirty face streaked with tears, was revealed staring into the lens. Behind her, pixelated palm trees were swaying under a pale sky. 'This message is for the attention of Doctor Jeremy Marrs, chairman of the International Science and Ethics Association . . .' She had an American accent, and it sounded as though she were reading the words from a board, off-camera. 'I'm contacting you because you know Jeff Hayden, and you need to know about his work at Geneflow Solutions—'

'And Josephs,' the voice cut in. 'Samantha Josephs is running things here.'

Adam had hoped he would never hear Josephs' name again. She was Hayden's right-hand woman; a brilliant but amoral scientist who could justify any action that got a desired result.

The frightened woman on the screen was trying to pick up where she'd left off. Adam was reminded of the horrible videos he'd seen on the news of soldiers captured by the enemy being forced to read their own ransom demands. 'Please, please, you *must* help us. There are lots of people trapped here. And creatures . . . It sounds crazy, but they're dinosaurs. Geneflow have bred dinosaurs. *Raptors*. They are smart. Deadly.' The woman shuddered visibly. 'One of them is helping us to survive – Loner here.' She sniffed noisily. 'We would've died a long time ago if not for him. He's going to try to send this from Geneflow's own computers. They . . . they don't know he can get inside their base.'

'Quickly,' hissed the eerie voice from off-camera, distorting the microphone. 'Brutes are coming . . .'

The woman's face twisted in fear as she spoke faster, gabbling in breathless sentences. 'We're on a tiny island in the Central Pacific, maybe six hundred kilometres south of Hawaii. There's a big concrete bunker here, used in World War Two, that's where the base is. There is also a place to land a boat that's marked with a stone pillar in the water. And a tower too . . .' She wiped her eyes and crouched down, barely in shot, as if afraid to be seen even by the camera. 'Please, please come . . .'

'Josephs and her kind are evil,' came the cold hiss of a voice. Adam felt a prickling through every hair in his body as the mass of red scales pushed back into sight and the focus blurred on a powerful, human-sized figure, half-lost in shadow.

Then the figure stepped back. Adam flinched and his father gripped the arms of his chair.

Confronting the camera, half in shot, was a reptilian nightmare. Though the picture lacked definition, those details he could see hit Adam like a stone. The beast's scaly skin was complicated about the shoulders by a sharp tangle of quills. Stubby feathers with a steely sheen coated the powerful arms. The neck was an obscenely thick gnarl of flesh, and the crimson-striped face a mash-up of vulture and crocodile with long, toothy jaws. On its hind feet, Adam could see a huge, sickle-shaped claw. The creature peered out from the screen with unblinking orange eyes. They were an animal's eyes, and yet the woman's grief seemed mirrored there.

The jaws creaked open. 'You must be here before the experiment ends.' The cold scrape of its voice filled and chilled the conference room. 'Before the feast.'

Then the screen switched to blank blue and a box that read NO SIGNAL. The creature's last word hung in heavy silence. The message had ended.

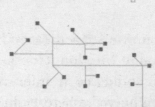

4: Stories Shared

For Adam, it seemed as though the night's chill had blown inside the conference room. *So it's starting again*, he thought bleakly. *The monsters. The fear.*

Mr Adlar asked for the message to be played through again. Chen worked the remote, but this time Adam looked away. He pictured Sam Josephs – black and bright, plain and petite. Nothing like the image of your typical evil mastermind. She looked so ordinary, but was reckoned to be an exceptional thinker; she'd worked her way into countless high-tech firms, stolen their secrets and fed them to Geneflow to speed its work along.

As the second viewing reached its chilling conclusion, Adam saw Chen's eyes flick between him and his father. 'Well, well,' the agent murmured. 'From the looks on your faces, anyone would think you really believe that crazy story the woman and her pet dinosaur are selling.'

'And so do you.' Mr Adlar took off his glasses and rubbed the bridge of his nose. 'Or else you'd hardly have bothered to abduct us in order to get a second opinion. That is why we're here, right?'

'Very astute, Mr Adlar.'

'Bill.'

'In your statement, Bill, you claim experience of "hyper-evolved reptile mutations",' said Marrs, quoting from a printout on the table in front of him. 'Agent Chen first contacted me a month ago, asking me if I could help with some enquiries he was making into the Geneflow organization. Naturally I remembered your anonymous statement . . .'

'And the details tallied with intelligence I'd gathered myself,' said Chen.

'What's wrong with you all?' Adam demanded, fear and dismay giving way to anger. 'We just heard about people dying, and that poor woman and a . . . a Z.raptor or something, and you're just sat there waving bits of paper like nothing's happened.'

'Easy, Adam.' Mr Adlar reached out a hand to place on Adam's shoulder.

'Easy?' Adam shrugged the fingers away. 'Geneflow have . . . I mean, they've . . .' He felt himself turning red as his voice began to choke on tears. 'Dad, they've started everything all over again.'

'We're not in this alone any more. Right?' Mr Adlar licked his lips. 'It's OK.'

Adam took some deep breaths, glaring at Marrs and Chen. 'Is it?'

'I assure you, we're taking this matter extremely seriously.' Marrs was as smooth and soothing as a practised politician. 'Agent Chen has been checking all leads – including your good selves. When he informed me he was ready to collect you both, I flew here from London on the next flight to discuss the matter further.' He paused, loosened his scarf a little as he turned to Mr Adlar. 'I was aware Hayden's research company was dabbling in cell-regeneration techniques, but can he really have created some sort of mutated reptile with the power of speech?'

'Yes,' said Mr Adlar simply. 'Geneflow accelerated the evolution of the original genetic pattern of a *Tyrannosaurus rex* in a very controlled way.'

'Right. They evolved ol' Rex all the way from a T to a Z, right?' Chen stretched. 'The project was codenamed Z. rex . . .'

I called him Zed, thought Adam.

'Josephs and Hayden tried to force me to help them control the Z. rex's thoughts and actions,' said Mr Adlar, 'using a system I'd actually designed for a new kind of videogame—'

'Ultra-Reality,' Adam put in. 'It's like you *feel* the

game. It turns your thoughts into computer code, and translates code back into brainwaves. You're right in there.'

'Intense,' drawled Chen without much enthusiasm.

'They held me prisoner for weeks,' said Mr Adlar. 'And to buy my obedience, they threatened to kill my son.'

'Assuming what you say is true, Bill,' said Chen, 'why in the world would they choose prehistoric wildlife to work with? I mean, sure, Hayden may have been a fossil hunter, but isn't that, like, making things way harder for themselves?'

'On the contrary,' Marrs said, 'I imagine it was the only viable option.' He leaned forward in his chair. 'We know certain species of dinosaur were the ancestors of modern birds. With cells from both animals available for study, you would have a start point and an end point. With enough computers to do the number-crunching, it ought to be possible to map out the sixty-six million years of genetic evolution between the two. With that information available, experts could divert the natural evolution of the dinosaur along *un*natural pathways, developing the physical make-up of the original species in whatever way they desired.' He nodded to himself. 'As a scientific achievement, it's incredible.'

'It's wrong,' Adam said quietly. 'We weren't meant to play with evolution like that.'

'What really worries me,' said Mr Adlar, 'is that the Z. rex was only the prototype of a living terror weapon. Geneflow were aiming to breed a whole army of them as part of a plan to create a new world order, or something . . .' Mr Adlar shook his head. 'It sounds crazy, like science fiction, I know. But Samantha Josephs certainly spoke of performing other experiments, developing other types of new-breed dinosaurs.' He looked at Chen. 'And you don't disbelieve me, do you? However much you might want to.'

'You said you'd gathered "intelligence" yourself,' Adam recalled. 'What d'you mean?'

'I've been investigating Josephs too,' Chen admitted, rubbing the back of his neck wearily. 'For instance – Bill, did you know that she used to work for your current employers, Mindcorp?'

'Yes,' Mr Adlar admitted. 'She spent a couple of months with them last year. I knew that.'

Adam looked at his dad in surprise. 'You did?'

'That's partly why I applied for a position there,' he admitted. 'Josephs specializes in stealing secret research from her employers. I wanted to know what she might have taken from Mindcorp, in case it cast light on Geneflow's other plans.'

'And does it?'

'Not that I can see.' Mr Adlar shrugged. 'The team at Mindcorp are creating the most detailed and accurate computer model of the human brain in existence. It'll help us understand the way the brain stores data and memory, how best to treat diseases that target the mind . . . Nothing to do with genetic evolution.' He looked at Chen suspiciously. 'What's the FBI's angle on this investigation?'

Chen sucked in his cheeks. 'I work out of the field office in Albuquerque, New Mexico. Back in August we received reports of a big explosion in the Fort Ponil region.'

I was there, thought Adam with a nervous glance at his dad. *Geneflow blew up their own base, trying to cover their tracks when they relocated to Edinburgh . . .*

'Our first thought was that this was some kind of terrorist activity,' Chen went on. 'An accident in a bomb-making factory, maybe. We looked into it . . . started excavating the site. By October we'd uncovered a secret laboratory complex, built right into the mountainside. The place was a wreck, but it was pretty clear we hadn't found ourselves a typical terrorist set-up. There were corpses – mostly thugs-for-hire and mercenaries, but some scientists too.' He swallowed hard, seemingly shaken by the memory. 'Some bodies had been crushed by an incredible pressure. Others were chewed on like beef jerky as if by some massive animal. Forensics thought we were playing a joke . . .'

No joke, thought Adam. *That was Zed, striking back at his creators.*

'Anyway, no leads on the next of kin for those bodies we could identify,' Chen went on. 'And most of the computers had been smashed or had all data wiped. But the forensics guys managed to scrape out a few names for investigation – Geneflow's, yours and Adam's, the Science and Ethics Association, Sam Josephs, this Z. rex thing – and a few notes about something called the Alta-Vita Unit . . .' He looked between the Adlars. 'That name mean anything to you?'

Mr Adlar shrugged. 'Never heard it before. *Vita* is Latin for "life", isn't it?'

'And *alta* means "high",' Marrs broke in. '*Ad alta*, for example, in Latin, would mean, *to the summit.*'

'The summit of life?' mused Mr Adlar.

'Well, anyway, I cross-referenced the names on the central database, and your anonymous report came up,' said Chen. 'Aside from Doctor Marrs's ethics committee you're the only person linked to the Z. rex project I've been able to trace.' He shook his head wearily. 'As an organization, it looks like Geneflow keeps itself and its employees well concealed.'

And everything else, Adam thought.

'Then this video gets sent,' Chen concluded. 'A new lead.'

'Who sent the email?' asked Mr Adlar.

'The sender was "LisaBee1972",' said Chen. 'That email account was set up six years ago by Lisa Brannigan, thirty-eight years old, resident of North Carolina. Barmaid in some spit 'n' sawdust joint. No kids or close family. She had an ex-husband, but he was executed by lethal injection in September of this year after eight years on death row.' He paused. 'Seems Lisa disappeared from home around the time of his execution. She's on the missing persons list. No one knows where she went, and no one's heard from her since.'

'Apart from me,' said Marrs, polishing his glasses on his scarf. 'Because it seems the woman in the video is undoubtedly Lisa Brannigan.'

Chen pushed a photocopied picture across the table. It showed a pale, friendly looking woman behind a bar. Adam felt a chill as he remembered the same face in the video, terror etched bone-deep on sunburned skin.

'What are you going to do?' he said simply.

'That is still to be decided,' Marrs said. 'But our priority is to build our case against Geneflow.'

'I'll say.' Chen looked down at the table. 'The sooner I know what's going down with Josephs and

Geneflow and their messing with the wildlife, the sooner I'll start sleeping nights again.'

I wouldn't be so sure. Adam thought of the red monstrosity rasping at the camera and shuddered. *I wouldn't bank on sleeping ever, ever again.*

5: Surprise Visitors

Adam stood in the dark room, his heart crawling slowly up his throat, feeling the ground tremble with the pound of giant footsteps. *He's coming. Any moment now . . .*

With a splintering crash the walls were torn apart and a huge, dark green monster stood illuminated in the glare of sudden, sweeping spotlights. Its jaws creaked open and choked up a syllable:

'Zed,' came the guttural grunt.

Adam took in the beast's appearance in scaly snatches. Legs as big as a man. Questing claws raking the air. A brute, massive head on a writhing neck, balancing the long tail that tapered behind. The monster opened its mouth and roared. Adam could actually feel the hot wetness of its stinking breath, saw the dark stains on its teeth and claws. He held still as the head pushed forward, and black, unblinking eyes swept over him. Then he reached out a hand and gingerly pressed it against the side of the creature's cold, dry cheek. It felt hard and lifeless.

'Zed,' the monster growled again.

Almost, thought Adam. *It's Dad's most impressive Ultra-Reality render yet. But it could never be as real as Zed was.*

'Quit,' he said out loud.

The dinosaur before him paused in the spotlights, flickering a fraction. 'Are you sure?' came a synthetic, female voice inside his head.

'Quit,' Adam said impatiently.

With a chime, the image faded from his eyes and he was back in his dad's room in the hotel, pulling the U-R headset from his face. He listened to his shaky breathing for a while, and the distant thrum of the traffic so many storeys below. He was back.

After a detailed discussion of their experiences with Geneflow, Adam and his dad had finally left the UN building close to eleven. Chen had driven them to the hotel in his cab. And although they were in the city that never slept, the pizza plans had been shelved. Neither Adam or his dad had felt hungry.

To escape the cold knot of fear pulling tighter in his belly, Adam had tried to immerse himself in the worlds of the prototype Ultra-Reality console. Slowly now, he peeled one of the system's sensor-pads from his forehead; and as he did so, he smudged a tear against his wrist.

The Think-Send system had been based on

Adam's own brainwaves, and as a result Zed had picked up something of the way Adam thought and felt. That – and the things they'd lived through – had created a bond between them. For as long as he lived, Adam would never forget the exhilarating fear of flying over the Atlantic while gripping the dinosaur's scaly skin, or the sickening horror of watching Zed battle his enemies to the death. The whole scenario could have been taken from some amazing game; no wonder his dad was trying to create a virtual Zed as a demo for U-R. But right now, the only thing that felt real for Adam was the cold, clammy question that refused to leave his head.

What's going to happen?

'Hey.' His dad came into the room, trying to act breezy. 'How's my super-gamer doing? Find any more glitches in the Zed demo?'

Adam shook his head and forced a smile. 'It's looking great, Dad.'

Mr Adlar sat down on the bed beside him. 'I'm surprised you want to spend any time close to dinosaurs right now.'

'I wouldn't mind having Zed here as a guard dog,' said Adam.

'I guess the cleaners might object,' said Mr Adlar wryly.

Adam didn't smile. 'I just want to feel safe again.'

'That won't happen until Geneflow is put out of business for good,' Mr Adlar reminded him. 'And maybe now we're getting a little closer to that happening.'

'Maybe.' Adam crossed to the window — not for the view of skyscrapers, shop fronts and water towers opposite, but for the advent calendar he'd balanced on the sill. He opened a cardboard flap and prised out the cheap chocolate within. 'I keep thinking of that poor woman, Lisa, trapped on an island with a whole load of those raptor things.'

Mr Adlar bumped the conversation on. 'I've been looking up raptors online, trying to see which species Geneflow have taken. It looked kind of like a *Velociraptor*, but they were not much bigger than a turkey. There were larger breeds, but—'

'Does it matter?' Adam shot back. 'We're talking about a *Z.* raptor. Josephs probably pumped it up to make it nastier.' He stared out over the city. 'And now it's being hunted down by Geneflow, just like Zed was.'

'Sounds as though this "Loner" can speak more easily than Zed could.' Mr Adlar shook his head. 'It makes me sick to think that Geneflow have used my technology to fill its brain. I wish to God I'd never met Sam Josephs.'

Adam regarded his father. 'Why didn't you tell me that she used to work at Mindcorp on that giant brain project? You're always saying how important it is that we're honest with each other.'

'I know, Adam. But you're my son and my instinct is to protect you. You're only thirteen—'

'I'm not *only* anything,' Adam snapped, then took a deep breath. 'But I am kind of glad you didn't uproot us from Scotland all over again just 'cause you fancied Christmas in New York.'

Mr Adlar shook his head. 'I never wanted any of this.'

'Can't you wave a magic wand or something? Make everything better?'

His dad considered. 'I could maybe wave the phone and have Room Service make us a late-night burger before bedtime. How would that be?'

Adam forced a smile and nodded. 'I suppose I could manage something.'

A sudden thumping on the suite's front door made them both jump.

'Wow, good Room Service,' Adam joked.

But Mr Adlar shushed him. 'Who knows we're here?' he whispered.

Adam felt an ice-cold dread rivet him to the spot.

'Bill?' came a familiar drawl through the door. 'It's cool, it's only me. John Chen.'

With a noisy puff of relief, Mr Adlar exited into the suite's living room to let him in, Adam just behind him. The door swung open to reveal Chen, hands shoved deep into the pockets of his black raincoat.

'What's up, Agent Chen?' said Mr Adlar coolly. 'I thought we were reconvening tomorrow?'

'That's right.' Chen smiled tightly. 'We just wanted a word in private.'

'We?' Adam echoed. Then he saw a tall, gaunt man follow Chen inside, a grey cap in his hand. Lexus man.

'I asked Doug to join us,' Chen explained, sitting on the couch without waiting to be asked. 'He's helping me out on this case. Doug Shanks, this is Bill Adlar. Adam you know already.'

'Uh-huh.' Doug shook hands with Mr Adlar and smiled at Adam. 'You gave me quite a workout.'

Adam looked down at his feet and said nothing. Doug took a seat in an armchair.

'I just got through talking with Doc Marrs again on the phone,' said Chen. 'He wants to play things his way, but I'm getting kinda worried about the timescale, you know?'

'How do you mean?' asked Mr Adlar.

'Well, he's set on digging up as much background information on Geneflow as possible, then he wants to present his findings to the UN Peacekeeping Operations Office of Military Affairs. They'll discuss the whole case to death over who knows how many weeks, and before they can send an international military force to the island it will have to be agreed by the General Assembly . . .'

Adam spoke up worriedly. 'And all the time, Geneflow will still be doing whatever they're doing.'

'Smart kid,' said Chen. 'Plus, how do we know your pal Hayden was the only Geneflow big cheese involved with the Ethics Association? If these guys find out that the UN are on to them . . .'

'They could go deeper into hiding, or bring their plans forward, or anything.' Mr Adlar sat down heavily in an armchair. 'So, what does the FBI plan to do?'

Chen smiled. 'I plan to let the doc get on with doing his thing. But in the meantime, we launch a reconnaissance mission. Try to find this island and Lisa Brannigan and get some hard proof of the deal with this dinosaur stuff. We've got a couple of good leads on which island Lisa Bee was talking about – a rough distance south of Hawaii . . . a crumbling tower visible from the sea . . .'

'Plus I've got a contact in Honolulu who runs long-distance boat tours round the big islands,' Doug put in. 'For an old pal and a couple of drinks, he might be able to point us in the right direction.'

Mr Adlar stared. 'This is how the FBI run their operations? Calling in favours from their agents' friends?'

Chen glanced at Doug with annoyance then

back at Adam's dad. 'I'm having to make this trip unofficial,' he admitted.

Mr Adlar stared. 'I don't understand.'

'I believe – I *know* – that someone in the Bureau has taken bribes from Josephs in the past to keep quiet about certain of her activities.' Chen got up and started to pace the room, agitated now. 'If we go after Geneflow by the book, things could get messy. That's why I'm going after Josephs now, without official sanction, and why I'm only taking along people I can trust. Like Doug here.' Chen looked Mr Adlar in the eye. 'And like you, Bill.'

'No,' Adam said at once.

Mr Adlar held up a hand to Adam, a 'calm down, I'll handle this' gesture. 'Agent Chen, no one wants to see Sam Josephs and Geneflow brought down more than me. But I've done what I can, told you all I know—'

'We need someone who understands something of the processes and technology involved,' Chen went on. 'Bill, you're an expert witness.'

'I'm a father,' Mr Adlar shot back. 'I'm not going to abandon my son while I go off scouring the ocean for Raptor Island.'

'Of course you're not,' said Chen reasonably. 'Because Adam's going to come with us.'

Adam stared in sick disbelief as Doug pulled a gun from his pocket. 'What the . . . ?'

'Run, Adam!' Mr Adlar grabbed a table lamp and hurled it at Doug. But the lamp was on too short a flex, it smashed on the floor before it got close to hitting Doug. As Adam charged for the door regardless, he heard a cold gasp of compressed air. Looking over his shoulder he saw his dad collapse over a coffee table. *Got to get help,* he thought, numb with horror as he reached the door. *Get to the front desk and get the police.*

But Doug was already aiming the pistol at him. *Phut!* Before Adam could even turn the handle, there was a sharp needle of pain in his side. He looked down to find a dart protruding from his ribs. A second later, his sight seemed to explode into vivid colours, flaring to whiteout as he crumpled silently to the floor.

6: Ocean Carnage

Adam woke from a pitching pit of blackness and wished he hadn't. His head felt like someone had set light to his brain and then stamped out the flames. Nausea turned through his aching stomach. His mouth was so dry he could hardly swallow. There was a sharp, slapping noise repeating in his ears and he struggled to make sense of it.

Sails, he thought numbly as the world lurched around him again. *Sails tugging in the wind. I'm on a boat.* Then he felt a sharp point scratch his arm, and gasped.

'You should start feeling a little more human soon,' came a deep voice beside him. 'You've been under sedation. Nothing to worry about, I kept a close eye on you the whole time.'

'You're a doctor?' Adam croaked.

'Yes. Or, used to be, anyway.'

Adam forced his eyes open. His vision was blurred but he saw a thin, dishevelled man sat just beside him in a tiny cabin, his beard greying faster than his thinning hair. He was holding something; a syringe? Adam's eyes flickered shut as his nausea got worse. His memories were hazy. He remembered someone helping him stumble off a plane at a tiny airport. The drone of men's voices as they gathered ina cabin, ignoring him at the back of the room. His dad, shouting that they be taken back to New York—

'Dad?' Adam's eyes snapped open again and he struggled to rise from the hard, narrow bunk he lay on. 'Dad! Where's my dad?'

'He's fine.' The bearded man fed him a little cool water, and gently eased him back to a supine position. 'He's on the other boat right now. John's with him.'

'John . . . *Chen* . . . ?' Suddenly events tangled back into Adam's mind. The violence in the hotel room. The video of the island. Lisa Brannigan – and the raptor. He grabbed the doctor's arm. 'I want to see my dad.'

'You will.' He gently but firmly removed Adam's fingers from his wrist. 'Very soon, I'm sure.'

Adam tried to slow his breathing. He felt weak and sick. 'Who are you people?'

'I'm Daniel Stone. Before I retired I was a forensic pathologist attached to the FBI.'

'A what?'

'I studied dead bodies to see how they died. Left

the Bureau under a bit of a cloud. John looked out for me. I owed him some favours, so . . .' He shrugged. 'It's the same for a lot of the guys on this trip. But this should help us pay him back.'

'Really?' Adam looked at him uneasily. 'Why did he take you, then? Is he expecting a lot of dead bodies?'

'Course not.' Stone smiled thinly. 'He just wanted a doctor on call for this trip. Better safe than sorry, right?'

Adam took some water in little sips. He stared around but could see only darkness through the little cabin's window. 'Where are we?'

'On a sailing ship called the *Hula Queen* in the Pacific Ocean, four days out of Honolulu.' Stone straightened. 'You know, a lot of the crew have been wishing they could swap places with you, they've been working their butts off—'

'Four days?' Adam echoed, incredulous. 'I've been sleeping all that time?'

'It was safe, no risk. And it seemed easiest all round.' A radio squawked in Stone's pocket, and he pulled it out. 'Hi, there. Yes, the boy's awake. No adverse reaction to the medication . . .' There was a brief snatch of garbled noise, which Stone made sense of at any rate. 'Right. We'll expect you.' He pushed the radio back into his pocket and smiled wanly at Adam. 'Agent Chen's coming over.

If you're feeling strong enough, he'd like to talk to you.'

I'd like to talk to him too, thought Adam hotly. But as he heard the thin, high rumble of an outboard engine from somewhere in the darkness outside, he felt suddenly afraid. His mind was still trying to make sense of his predicament. He'd blacked out in a hotel room in Manhattan and come round on the other side of the world in the middle of the Pacific . . .

'Why wake me now?' he demanded suddenly. 'Why after all this time?'

'Because we've found it,' said Stone. 'The island.'

Raptor Island. Adam's nausea got suddenly worse. 'No,' he breathed hoarsely. 'No, we can't be there.'

'Come on. Take it slowly.' Stone gave Adam some more water, took hold of his arm and helped him to stand. The floor was shifting with the swell of the ocean, but Adam held it together and managed to reach the door by himself. He opened it and shuffled into a narrow corridor, which in turn led to a flight of steps stretching up to the deck.

Woozily, with a little help from Stone, he scaled the staircase and rested in the doorway. Above decks, the air was sharp and fresh; it helped to clear his head.

The first thing he noticed was that the ship was big; the deck was almost as wide as a typical classroom and maybe four times as long. It was lit with red lanterns, turning the handful of crew into crimson silhouettes as they scrambled about on deck and in the rigging. One of them was Doug, his familiar grey cap still in place; Adam took a step back on instinct. Staring past the shadow-figures, Adam searched out the blurred split between boundless black sea and starry night. With a slow tingle of dread he made out a low hump of distant darkness beneath the pale disc of the moon.

'I might not have seen it at all, if not for the tower,' Doug called, and Adam saw what he meant – an ungainly stack of stone thrust up at the stars. 'Not long now till we bag ourselves a monster, guys. Its head's gonna look good on the wall of the vets' club . . .'

'What do we do with the rest of the thing?' someone else asked.

'Barbecue!' Doug declared. 'Bet you that monster tastes sweet.'

'It'll taste like charcoal, the way you cook it.'

Laughter rang out into the empty darkness, and Adam's heart began to pound helplessly. He was glad that Stone at least wasn't smiling.

Then the whine of an outboard motor stole into Adam's ears; he turned to find a small, sleek orange boat was skimming over the white-crested waves from out of the shadow of another large sailing ship.

'Your dad's quartered on the *Pahalu* there,' Stone said, coming up behind him. 'I brought him round yesterday. He's fine. If a little . . . aggrieved.'

'I want to see him,' Adam said.

'You'll have to talk to Chen.'

Nerves balled in Adam's stomach as he saw Chen at the helm of the powerboat pulling up alongside the *Hula Queen*.

'Hey, Adam,' he called up, his oriental features half in shadow. 'Welcome back.'

A big guy in a red T-shirt came up and flipped a steel rope-ladder over the side of the ship. Adam watched coldly as Chen climbed up. 'You kidnapped my dad and me.'

'I'm sorry. I needed your dad, Adam, and I couldn't leave you home alone in case Geneflow came looking. You're a lot safer here, believe me.' Chen swung his legs over the side of the ship and pulled a radio from his pocket. 'Go ahead and talk to your old man. Press down the button on the side when you want to speak.'

Without comment, Adam seized the radio. 'Dad, are you there?'

'Adam! Are you all right, Adam?' His dad's voice sounded strong and vibrant even over the tinny speaker. 'Don't be afraid, OK? It's going to be fine.'

Adam glared at Chen as he talked. 'I want to see you, Dad. Why have they split us up?'

'To keep you safe,' his dad said. 'You're staying on that ship with Doctor Stone and a minder, well away from the island. As for me . . . I'll be going ashore with the second group.'

'Second group?' said Adam numbly, still trying to catch up as the situation raced on around him.

'Sure.' Chen pulled a pair of night-vision binoculars from his pocket and trained them on the island. 'I'm leading the first expedition ashore in the RIBs.' He must've noticed Adam's blank look. 'Rigid Inflatable Boats, like that one I took over here. We'll land discreetly, check out the area, and if it's safe . . .' He pointed to the bigger ship. 'We'll bring in the *Pahalu* there. She's a whole lot more defendable than the RIBs in case we need to make a quick getaway.'

'And what are you going to do once you're on the island?' Adam demanded.

'If Lisa Brannigan and the other people trapped there are still alive, they'll need help,' said Chen, tucking the binoculars away again. 'From the look of things, better help than that talking dinosaur can offer. We're bringing medical care as well as muscle.'

'You're acting like you're such a good guy.' Adam realized his thumb was still on the transmit button, sending the conversation to his dad.

As he released it, Mr Adlar's voice gusted out: 'Chen, I'm begging you to think again about this madness. Call for proper back-up before it's too late . . .'

As Adam's dad railed on, Chen turned down the volume and beckoned over the guy in the red T-shirt. 'Brad, try to take us in a little closer to the island. The outboards on the RIBs are noisy – the less we need to run them, the better.' As Brad took off to chivvy the crew and weigh anchor, Chen put the radio back to his mouth. 'Are you through acting like my mother, Bill?'

'You saw those creatures on the video,' Mr Adlar went on, 'but you don't know what they're really capable of.'

'And you don't know what my friends here can do,' Chen retorted. The *Hula Queen* lurched as the wind caught in her sails, propelling her onwards towards the island. 'Thirteen highly trained, heavily equipped hunters, all pros – ex-cops or military. We have enough firepower to take out a small army and get us access to Josephs and the rest.' He took a deep breath. 'We'll be going in shortly, Bill. Sit tight. I'll contact Rich when I can to give the all clear to come and join us.'

'Can't you let Dad stay here on this boat too?' Adam pleaded. 'You could talk to him on the radio if you need to.'

'I'm sorry, but I need him with me to ID what-ever crazy science stuff they've got going down here.' Chen looked haunted, caught between the eerie red glow of the lanterns and the night. 'I need to know what Geneflow are really doing. Josephs can snow me, but not your dad. He knows the score.'

Adam stared helplessly at the receding silhouette of the *Pahalu* and then back at Chen. 'Why is it so important you-know what Josephs is doing?'

'All *you* need to know is that when this is all over, I'll let you and your dad go free.' Chen looked out to the island, which was maybe a couple of kilometres away now and growing steadily nearer. 'I'm going to make things right here. Whatever it takes . . .'

He'd barely finished talking when a blow came from the other side of the boat – a sudden, violent jolt that sent everyone sprawling. Chen grabbed the rail as he fell and barely stopped himself from being flung over the side. A deep, splintering noise sounded in the darkness.

'We've hit something!' Doug shouted. 'Could be we've run aground on a reef . . .' He was already sprinting to the other side of the boat. But the next jolt was even more extreme, slamming him to the deck as the boat listed sideways and lurched drunkenly through the waves.

A huge spray of water lashed overhead and Adam slipped and fell, dragging Stone down with him to the wet wood. To his horror, he saw that the side of the boat had already dipped so low that water was gushing across the deck.

Stone put Adam's fears into words succinctly: 'We're sinking!'

Chen had pressed the radio back to his lips. 'Rich, we just struck something,' he said tersely. 'Coral, maybe. Keep the *Pahalu* well back. We'll evacuate in the RIBs and join you.' He shoved the radio into his pocket and shouted to his crew. 'Brad, Doug, do what you can to hold her steady. The rest of you, into the RIBs, come on! Stone, watch out for the kid.'

Adam helped Stone to his feet. 'I'm starting to wish you hadn't woken me after all.' Two men pushed past them, vaulting the rail where Chen had come aboard, plunging down into the black water beside the orange RIB. Adam watched them scramble inside and bit his lip. 'We have to do that?'

'We can use the ladder,' Stone said, leaning heavily on the rail. 'I— I'll go first, show you it's safe.'

'OK,' said Adam. He could see the two men were inside the boat now, urging Stone to join them. The old man wasn't moving, except for the tremble in his hands.

Then Adam saw why. 'Agent Chen!' he yelled.

The water below was churning white as a dark shape – easily as long as a two train carriages –

broke the surface maybe twenty metres from the RIB and the *Hula Queen*. 'Oh . . . my . . . God . . .' He glimpsed a hideous reptilian head as large as a couch, sharp bestial features warped and twisted. Jutting sails of flesh that might have been fins struck out from its glistening, grey-black body.

'What is that thing?' hissed Stone.

'It's heading straight for the boat.' Adam remembered in New York he'd wished for Zed as a guard dog to keep people away. Had Geneflow followed the same line of reasoning . . . ?

'Get away from here!' Chen yelled down to his men. 'Go! Go!'

Too late. The sleek orange RIB and its horrified passengers were snatched away in a churning explosion of white foam.

'No!' Chen shouted, his voice cracking.

And then the massive creature burst up from the darkness and towered over the stricken vessel. Adam held stock still, unable even to breathe. The creature was no dinosaur. It resembled some colossal, long-necked sea-serpent with gigantic, pointed jaws. Yellow slit-eyes glowing, it spat bloody splinters of wood and orange plastic in all directions before crashing back down into the water.

Chen was already back on his radio. 'Rich, turn tail, get the *Pahalu* out of here and stay on this frequency for word from me.' There was a brief squawk of protest and static. 'No buts! Stay here and you'll be sunk like the *Hula*, there'll be nothing you can do to help.'

Stone clutched frantically at Chen's shirt. 'What about us?'

Pulling free angrily, he pointed to where Doug and Brad were wrestling with a kind of steel cradle holding another of the fluorescent landing craft. 'We're carrying two RIBs ourselves, remember?' There was a roar of straining metal, and one end of the craft slipped on its chain, hurtling seawards. Then it jammed, the boat hanging at an angle above the water.

Swearing, two more men grabbed at the other end of the cradle. 'Come on,' Chen told Adam and Stone, and ran over to lend his weight. But before he'd even got halfway, the ship shook again under some colossal impact and a massive wave crashed down over the deck. The rush of water knocked the special agent over the side of the ship before he could even scream for help.

'Chen's overboard!' Doug shouted. 'Life vest, someone!'

The radio's gone with him, thought Adam helplessly. *My only link to Dad*. Spying the bulky orange vest hanging up across the deck, he realized he was closest and ran to fetch it, almost tripping over loose ropes as he went.

'Give me that.' Doug slipped and skidded across the pitching deck to grab the life vest from Adam, then staggered back to where Chen had fallen. 'No sign.' He hurled it helplessly it into the darkness. 'Chen!'

Adam pointed out two more vast shapes in the moonlit water, incoming like giant torpedoes. 'There's more of those things coming!' he cried, as the whole ship almost turned upside down with the force of the blow. Rails buckled and the wooden floor split. Dr Stone was catapulted into the darkness, his scream eclipsed by a ferocious roar from one of the things in the water.

'Come on, kid.' Doug gripped Adam by the arm and propelled him towards the RIB, knocked free of its cradle by the impact and slipping down into the water. Panic-stricken, some of the crewmen were jumping after it. But Brad had grabbed a rifle from a large wooden crate and fired down into the water, yelling over the blazing rattle of automatic gunfire.

'That's no good!' Doug bawled in his face, wrestling the gun away. 'Help me get the crate in the second RIB, we can give everyone weapons . . .'

Soaked through and freezing, Adam turned and saw the shadow of the *Pahalu* drifting serenely away from them into the darkness. 'Dad, don't leave me!' he screamed.

Then the boat lurched again and threw Adam backwards. He toppled from the deck and smashed into freezing saltwater. Stunned, he accidentally swallowed, burning his nose and throat. He choked in the darkness, felt something hard brush against him. Panicking, he pushed upwards, broke the surface, gulped down air. One of the RIBs was bobbing ahead of him. Someone grabbed him by the neck of his T-shirt and hauled him into the crowded boat. More men were floundering in the water, arms windmilling, shouting in terror as massive fins scythed through the water close by. Adam saw some of them swimming desperately for the hunched shadow of the island in the far distance, saw the *Hula Queen* looming up beside him – or what was left of it.

Staring in awestruck horror he watched as two of the enormous sea-creatures rose from the water, tearing into the hull in a frenzy, ripping out wood and metal with serrated, saw-blade teeth.

Then a deep, creaking noise high above them warned of fresh danger. Adam saw a long, narrow shadow swing across the stars – one of the masts from the *Hula Queen* slowly toppling like a felled tree, ready to fall and crush them all. Desperately, he tried to dive from the boat, but others were trying to do the same, jostling and blocking his way. He lost his balance, fell back with a gasp. Men trampled him in the darkness. The RIB had become a pit of bodies writing in cold saltwater.

You don't know what my friends here can do, Chen had said so proudly.

They can die, thought Adam, all hope of escape gone now. He heard the grating roar of the sea monsters, the yawning creak of the falling timber. Then something hit him across the back of the head, and black, unforgiving night descended.

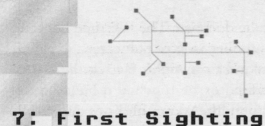

7: First Sighting

Adam jerked awake from the blackness of his sleep into strong, burning daylight. He was soaking wet. His head was pounding and his lips felt cracked and swollen; he licked them and almost choked on the salty taste. He held very still, lying on his back on wet sand, concentrating on the hiss and lap of the sea in his ears.

A single question arrowed through his mind: *Where's Dad?*

As the events of last night began to drip back into his memory, Adam dimly recalled someone hauling him out of the RIB as it scraped onto the shore. Exhausted after so many days' sedation, he'd blacked out again soon after. Even now he just wanted to curl up and go back to the dark. He didn't feel ready to face the truth of his situation.

I'm stranded. Me and the wildlife . . . and who else? Adam's eyes snapped open and he flinched from the harsh light.

He was lying on a beach maybe a hundred

metres long, bookended by rocky outcrops. Looking up, he saw an unbroken line of palm trees, shielding the rest of the island from sight. He felt the top of his head and winced as he touched a huge bruise, its centre etched with the wet crumble of a scab. His fingers came away bright red; he grimaced but the injury didn't seem too bad. *That falling mast must have connected with other people before it got me*, he realized.

So where was everyone? There were churned up tracks in the sand, leading to the tree line. Others must have survived, but where had the RIBs vanished to?

He pictured the sea monsters tearing apart the *Hula Queen*. Was his dad still safe on Chen's other ship? Would he be trying to get to the island, to find Adam? Or since Chen had fallen into the water, maybe 'Rich' would've cut his losses and just turned and left . . .

Adam stared out over the glittering turquoise sea ranged before him. Debris from the *Hula Queen* bobbed on the gentle waves or lay strewn across the beach: pieces of timber, clothes, plastic boxes, a length of rope.

Then Adam realized there were bodies in the water too.

With a sick feeling he waded out toward the nearest figure. It was floating face down, the upper body tangled in a length of sail. Holding his breath, he pulled at the thick, sodden material. That drew the body towards him, and he retreated squeamishly. As he did so, the scrap of sail pulled loose and he recognized the grey cap still wedged over the head. It was Doug. Adam tried to turn the bloated body over. It seemed to weigh a ton. Water streamed from the man's open mouth, and Adam almost retched. He felt tears ball in his throat. He'd hardly known Doug, and the memories weren't exactly to be cherished. But to see the man dead, and to know how terrible his last moments must've been . . .

Anger swamped Adam, heightened by his rising despair. 'Hope you're happy, Agent Chen,' he muttered. 'If you aren't dead already.' He towed the lifeless body through the water to shore, then headed out again to ID the next body, dread weighing down every step. He saw another man floating on his back, dead eyes baking in the sun.

Mechanically, he manhandled the body up onto the beach – he recognized him as one of the deck hands. Then he began to shake. The scale of his predicament was burning through him, hotter than the sun on his skin. He was stranded and alone on Raptor Island, completely cut off from the world outside. Whatever had trashed the *Hula Queen* would still be patrolling the waters. And surely

Geneflow would know about the wreck by now? They were bound to come looking.

But even as he reflected on those dangers, the memory of the hideous red raptor-creature calling for help spread through his head like blood through water. It was here, somewhere, with him and who knew what other horrors — all of them crowded together on a tiny speck in the sea.

Adam blinked away his tears and wiped snot from his top lip. He'd been caught in life-or-death situations before; there was no way he was going to give up now. And none of the wreckage in the water seemed to hail from the *Pahalu*, so that gave him hope. He stood up straight. First, he had to find his fellow survivors. Maybe Chen had been one of those who'd swum for it and found his way to shore. Maybe his radio had survived intact too. If they all stuck together, watched out for each other . . .

Suddenly, a rustling, crashing noise carried from the dense tree line behind him. Adam turned, his heart lurching. There was no cover out here on the beach, nowhere to hide—

But it was only a man in a torn red T-shirt. Chen's friend, Brad, burst out of the thick foliage. His clothes were in tatters, soaked dark with blood. His staring eyes were wild as he took in Adam and stopped running for a moment. But the crashing from the trees hadn't stopped. Brad turned in terror to look at whatever was coming after him – and a colourless jet of fluid spat from the undergrowth, catching him full in the face. Brad screamed, an awful, high-pitched noise, and fell to his knees, clawing at his eyes.

'Help me!' he yelled, as the skin on his face started bubbling with gruesome blisters. 'I can't see! I can't see!'

The cries jolted Adam into action. He started to run over.

But then a monster pushed out from the foliage.

Adam skidded to a stop. Just fifty or so metres away there stood a massive, hulking creature, a few strides from the screaming Brad. Staring intently. Salivating.

A dinosaur.

Time slowed as the beast burned into Adam's senses. It was different from the raptor in the video: bulkier, clay-grey, as tall and broad as two men. Its eyes were dark and narrowed. The snout was long like a crocodile's, the jaws crammed with a way-ward mess of ivory spikes that looked strong enough to tear through metal. Its thick, upright torso was balanced on stocky, muscular legs and its long, ridged neck was balanced by an even longer tail, coiling and twitching as though it had life of its own. Adam's eyes flicked between the long, blade-like claws on the ends of the monster's twitching fingers and the hooked talons curving up from its hind legs, and his skin crawled like it had places to go.

The monster sniffed and switched its attention from Brad to Adam. Adam felt sick. Zed had been a much larger beast and way more powerful, and yet there was something more unsettling about this monster. It might have been the way the traditional dinosaur form was roughed up with a shock of short, steel-grey feathers over the arms, shoulders and chest, knitting together into a kind of weird chain mail, like it had dressed to kill. Or the way it held itself so still, the drool pooling from its mouth the only movement – a deadly, decisive hunter, assessing its prey.

'Help me, somebody!' Brad screamed, his face blistered red and swollen. Adam wanted to help, but with the beast so close he didn't dare. The giant raptor began to sway on its hind legs, back and forth. It ground its monstrous, mismatched teeth together, a noise like nails scraping a chalkboard, as a low growl built in its throat. Brad crawled blindly forwards on his knees through the sand, arms out-stretched, making for the sea. With a howl of triumph, the monster behind him pounced, kicking up huge sprays of sand as it leaped forward, the thick neck stretching and the jaws swinging wide as it bore down on its helpless victim.

Adam turned, sick with fear, and the crunch and crack of splintering bone was like a starter's pistol firing off his flight. He ran, panic-stricken, tearing over the wet sand towards the outcrop that marked the end of this little bay. He had no idea what lay on the other side but there was no other option.

He knew too that there would be nowhere to hide. The giant creature was slobbering over its kill and Adam knew it would come for him next. It had no need to rush. It would take him out with a jet of that acidic spray and catch him with ease. It could cover the same ground as Adam in a fraction of the time, and when it caught him . . .

Adam half-climbed, half-scrambled over the rocky outcrop, the surf slapping against his ankles, the sharp stone scraping his palms. On the other side he found another empty stretch of beach, littered with clothes and debris from the wreck. No bodies here. *Keep it that way*, he thought, forcing himself to move faster.

As he jumped down onto the beach and started towards the tree line, another of the hideous creatures crashed out from the dense vegetation. It was darker, larger, its head scarred with thick scratches. Adam veered away as the giant raptor spat its own spray of colourless liquid metres through the air. Most of the acid missed, but a little splashed against his bare ankle and he shouted as he felt a surge of pain and heat. But adrenaline kept back the worst of the burn, his body urging him to focus only on his plight, on his *flight*, on getting away. There had to be somewhere on this island that was safe.

Or off *this island* . . .

Adam could hardly believe it. Drifting lazily into sight across the calm ocean was one of the RIBs, a vision in fluorescent orange, just fifty metres or so from shore. The *Hula Queen's* name was printed on its side — the lapping waves must have coaxed it from the shore-edge back out into the waters or else perhaps it was the other boat, washed in from the open sea . . .

Adam heard an ear-splitting roar from the outcrop he'd just negotiated as the first raptor made its proximity known. *I know how fast they can move on land*, he thought. *But how fast can they swim?* He ran into the ocean, but the water soon slowed his steps, so he dived forward and started swimming for his life with his most powerful front crawl. There was a titanic splash behind him. The raptors were following. Could they swim? He had no idea.

But he guessed he would find out.

Breath catching in his throat, saltwater burning his eyes, Adam quickened his stroke. If he could only get inside and get the outboard motor started . . .

He risked a backward glance. Big mistake. The creatures were gaining — their muscular legs powering them through the water. He tried to push himself harder, moaning with fear. *Come on. Come on!* The orange craft was so close . . .

But then suddenly, a throaty, aggressive whine spluttered and rose into the air. *The motor*, Adam realized, *starting by itself . . . ?*

'No!' he screamed with the last of his strength as his only hope began gliding away from him. 'Come back!' The crashing in the water behind grew louder, more ferocious. Adam kept swimming though he knew in his heart now it was hopeless. His arms were starting to cramp. A jet of burning spit struck his shoulder, and he cried out as his skin blistered. Flipping round onto his back he found that the two behemoths were almost on top of him, claws clacking, tails thrashing through the water, their jaws gaping open in grisly grins, pushing down towards him, ready to devour.

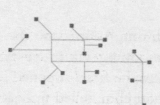

8: Finding Harmony

The triumphant roar of the raptors snatched all other sound away from Adam's ears. His only warning that a signal flare had been fired was when an explosion of flame and red smoke detonated in the mouth of the nearest monster. The creature fell back, snarling, frothing and choking smoke. Its brother retreated in alarm, hooting and swinging its great, grey head.

'*Get in!*'

Adam turned at the shrill call, and found the lifeboat had turned back towards him, a dark-skinned girl at the tiller. 'Come on,' she urged him, waving the flare gun.

Whoever she was, she'd saved his life. New hope lending him strength, Adam forced himself to struggle on towards the boat.

Steering with one hand, the girl reached over the side with the other and took hold of his wrist, towing him away. While the injured raptor bit and snapped at the seawater to extinguish the smoke and fire in its throat, Adam saw the other raptor gnashing its overgrown teeth in frustration – eager to kill but afraid of the fire. It opened its jaws and a loud, grating groan channelled from its throat.

Adam could have sobbed with relief as the RIB powered out of range of the killers, moving westwards until the stretch of beach was far behind. It felt so good to be just pulled along through the warm water, a passive passenger, the girl's grip on his wrist strong and—

Then the moment's release was lost as his rational side took hold in a clamour of questions. 'Who are you? I thought this boat was empty. Where did you—?'

'Whoa there.' She cut the engine and turned to him, offering him her other hand. 'You'd better get inside. And then, how about you try saying thank you?'

He gripped hold of her other hand as she helped him clamber over the side and he splashed down onto the blood-stained wooden floor. 'Thanks,' he said with feeling. 'You saved my life. I'm sorry I—'

'S'OK,' she said, her voice seasoned with a hard American twang. 'Raptors are a good excuse for forgetting your manners. Shame that gun was only packing the one flare, or I'd have given both of them a smoking.' She paused. 'I'm Harm.'

He looked at her blankly.

'Harm short for Harmony.' She rolled her eyes. 'Sucks as a name, right?'

'I'm Adam.' He realized he was still hanging onto her hand so he shook it, screwing up his eyes against the sun's glare. 'I was on a ship, it was attacked.'

'Last night, I know. Saw you go down.' She mimed a pair of binoculars to her eyes, then lowered them.

Adam's relief took a smack to the guts as he was hit by sudden doubt. The girl looked half-starved, a real survivor — but what if she was part of a trick, someone sent out by Geneflow to pick up any survivors? To pick up *him* specifically? He decided he would play a little dumb for a while, not give away what he knew, or how he'd come to be here.

'There've been a few wrecks,' Harm went on. 'Lucky for you it seems to be the ships the monsters attack, not the people. Even luckier, the raptors didn't sniff you out as soon as you washed up on shore.'

Adam sat so the sun wasn't in his eyes and he could see Harm-short-for-Harmony properly. She was a littler older than he was, the soft lines of her face hardened by experience, her skin darkened nearly black by the tropical sun. Her hair was long and clumsily braided, held off her forehead by a wide, grimy white band. She looked painfully thin;

bony ribs poking from beneath her cropped sky-blue top and legs like sticks from her cut-off jeans. She wore a tatty white satchel on a strap over one shoulder, but it looked empty.

She shifted uncomfortably. 'What's the matter? You were expecting maybe Robinson Crusoe?'

'I'm sorry.' Adam realized he'd been staring. 'I didn't know anyone was in the lifeboat when I swam out to it.'

'That's 'cause I didn't want *them* to see me,' she explained. 'I was looking for anything useful that washed in.'

'Glad that included me.'

'Not so sure it does, yet.'

Adam half-smiled and looked around edgily, wondering what to do. As he did so, he saw a dark-red figure standing on a cliff top; a smaller raptor, like the one in the video. As he tensed, it turned and bolted, vanishing from sight.

To tell others? Or to trail them more discreetly?

He looked out to sea. *Oh, Dad, why aren't you here?*

As the boat bobbed over a wave, something rolled against Adam's fingers. It was a half-full bottle of water, caked in sand. Thirsty after his ordeal, he automatically pulled off the top to swig from it.

But Harm snatched it from his grip. 'Are you crazy?'

'What?' he asked. 'I haven't drunk anything since last night.'

'I haven't drunk anything since lunch time yesterday,' she informed him. 'There's no fresh water on this island. So this is like gold, got it? You can have a sip. Just one for now, 'K?'

'Sure.' Adam gingerly took back the bottle and wet his lips. Harm took the bottle from him, hesitated, then took a tiny gulp. She closed her eyes and shook a little, savouring the taste. Then quickly she resealed the bottle and pushed it under her seat. 'It's going to be that much harder now,' said Harm, 'picking up stuff from those beaches. Place will be crawling with raptors. And we need all the supplies we can get.'

'We?'

'My group.'

Adam raised his eyebrows. 'Are there lots of you here?'

'Not any more. We're down to three – four, counting you.'

Adam shifted in his seat uneasily. 'How long have you been here?'

'Three months.'

Three months? Adam tried to imagine a quarter of a year, trapped in a place where absolutely everything was set on killing you.

She fixed him with her dark eyes. 'Your accent.

Sounds like you came a long way. How many on your boat?'

'I'm not sure. Mostly American. I'm from the UK, though my dad's from Chicago . . .' He changed the subject. 'You said *your* group. Are there other groups hiding out here?'

'Some, maybe.'

'You don't know?'

Harm looked at him oddly. 'No. Hiding is the name of the game here. A smaller crowd attracts less attention from the raptors, makes you harder to hunt.' She weighed the oar in her hands. ''Cause round here you never know what's going to be coming after you . . .'

Suddenly she brought the oar down hard on the side of the boat, missing Adam's fingers by millimetres. He snatched his hand away, stared at her. 'What the—?'

She leaned forward aggressively. 'You just got here last night, you get chased by two king-sized dinosaurs about to chow down on your butt and when I save you, all you wanna know is how many people on the island. Are you a spy or something, working for *them*?'

'No!' Adam protested. 'No way!' Harm swung the oar again. The flat side hit his burned shoulder and he cried out in pain. 'I didn't talk about the dinosaurs because I probably know more about them than you do. And how do I know *you're* not working for Geneflow Solutions?'

Harm stared. 'You know about Geneflow?'

'Too much,' Adam told her shakily. 'I know they're turning dinosaurs into living weapons. I'm only here now because of the video begging for help to come here.'

She held the oar still raised. 'Video?'

'It was made by a woman called Lisa – and a Z. raptor.'

Adam was gratified by the startled reaction on Harm's gaunt face.

'So Loner wasn't lying,' she said. 'He really did know how to get word outside.'

'You know Lisa?'

'She's part of the group,' said Harm. 'It was her camera they used to shoot the movie. She's been like a mom to me.'

'And what about Loner?'

'We haven't seen him for days.' Harm looked troubled. 'I guess he could be dead. He was always afraid the other raptors would find out he's been helping the humans.'

'Why *has* he helped you?'

She shrugged dourly. 'He says him and us are all outsiders. We need to stick together. And without his protection . . .'

'It's possible there's a little more protection

coming,' said Adam. 'On that ship there was an FBI agent, a doctor, a whole bunch of hunters and hard men—'

'FBI?' Harm's eyes grew wider. 'And hunters? So there were weapons on board?'

'A whole crateful. But I don't know what happened to them. I saw footprints on the shore, I think some of the men made it. Unless the raptors got them.'

Harm hardly seemed to be listening any longer, though at least she put down her oar. 'If we could only get our hands on real weapons . . .'

'How many people does Geneflow have here?' asked Adam.

'I dunno. We never see them. Only Loner's seen inside their base. It's hidden away underneath the military ruins – ruins at the heart of the Vel settlement.'

'Vel?'

'*Velociraptor*, I mean. Like Loner.' She rubbed her eyes. 'See, there's two kinds of raptor here on the island and they hate each other's guts. Vels are smaller and fast. Brutes are big and dumb – they're the ones who were chasing you. Killers.'

Adam raised his eyebrows. 'And the *Velociraptors* aren't?'

'Sometimes they kill. But mostly they catch people, keep them locked up, make them do stuff.'

She started rowing, rangy muscles bunching and gliding on her skinny arms. 'Loner says they make them slaves or something.'

'Loner's really helping you?'

'He's not like the other Vels. He's smarter, you know? A better talker.' She shrugged. 'Maybe that's why he's tried to look out for us.'

Adam put his head in his hands. 'And does Loner have any idea why Geneflow have put two lots of mega-evolved raptors on some tiny island and left them to it?'

'For fun?' Harm's voice dripped with sarcasm. 'David says it's got to be some kind of experiment.'

'David?'

'He's taken charge of our group. Used to be a teacher – leading the class is in his blood, I guess.' She pointed to another oar at the side of the boat. 'Come on, help. I still don't know if you're on the level, but David needs to hear what you've got to say.'

'OK.' Adam took the oar, tested his muscles, and didn't like the result. 'Can't we turn the engine back on?'

'Too risky. Raptors would hear us coming.'

Adam looked over at the island coastline. It looked so deceptively calm and peaceful. He thought he saw something move among the trees; a shift of red scales, brilliant sunlight flashing off a monstrous claw.

Then nothing.

Raptors on the land and monsters in the sea, he reflected. *Between them, we're well and truly trapped.*

Shivering, Adam paddled harder through the turquoise waters, as if the physical strain could drive the dread-filled thoughts from his mind.

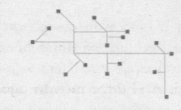

9: The Survivors

After half an hour of sweaty, sunburned effort, Harm put down her oar. Adam saw a weathered pillar of concrete rising from the water beside a rocky outcrop – a sign that here the sea was deep enough for a larger boat to attempt a mooring.

'This is the landing point. It's close to our latest camp.' Harmony stared into the trees. 'But Lisa said she saw Brutes round here yesterday.'

'What dinosaur breed are the Brutes?' wondered Adam. 'Do you know?'

'You sure got a thirst for knowledge, don't you? Bet David would've loved you in his class.' She went on scrutinizing the scenery. '*Utahraptor*, Loner said. That's where David got our name for them – you know, *Utahraptor*, Brute-a-raptor. Funny, huh?' She shook her head. 'Sometimes I could just die laughing. I'm from Utah too.'

'You are?'

'Weber County.' Harm stretched her arms, massaging the muscles after their workout. 'Wasatch

Mountains seem a long way away now. I always figured that would be a good thing. Spent most of my life waiting to leave.'

Adam nodded. 'And three months ago, you did, right?'

'I'm fifteen, but I've got a fake ID that says I'm seventeen,' Harm explained. 'I was on a plane, with Lisa and David and a whole bunch of others. The pilot said something went wrong. He put us down here.'

'On this tiny island in the middle of nowhere?'

'There's a runway, and a couple of roads. Stuff left over from the Second World War or something.' A haunted look stole into her eyes. 'The pilot took off again without us. Before we'd even seen what was lying in wait here. Guess we'll never know why.'

'So this place is on some airline's flight path?' Adam felt faint hope stir his insides. 'Where were you headed?'

'The airstrip's been destroyed since then,' Harm said curtly. 'Blown to bits, nothing can land there now. So don't get your hopes up.' Abruptly she picked up the oar and started propelling the RIB towards the rock-pile jetty. 'Enough talk already. I *think* the way's clear.'

With that qualifier hanging large in his mind, Adam joined in with the rowing.

As they pulled up alongside the jetty, he kept breaking off to feel the back of his neck and shoulder, wincing as he did so.

'Brutes sprayed you, huh?' Harm whispered, looping a mooring rope over a wooden post. 'You're lucky you washed it off pretty fast. Brutes spit that stuff from their guts. It turns flesh and bone to slush. Means they can eat just about anything. No waste.'

'Did you ever think about becoming a tour guide, Harmony?' Adam said. 'You really make a place come alive.'

'Better hope this particular place stays dead a little longer.' She shot him a sideways glance. 'And I told you – it's Harm.'

'I know.' He shrugged and smiled. 'Sounds kind of dangerous.'

She didn't smile back. 'Mess with me and it will be.'

Feeling a little foolish, Adam climbed out of the lifeboat after her. The jetty creaked and shifted alarmingly, but held their weight as they moved onto a sandy, grassy path that wound up a steep hillside. Harm was walking barefoot; thick calluses cushioned her feet. She stopped to pull a plant from a rock and shove it into her mouth.

'What's that?'

'Food. Sea purslane. Want some?'

He shook his head.

'Choosy, huh?' She wiped her mouth and an almost-smile caught at her lips. 'We'll see how long that lasts.'

'Is that why this David sent you out foraging for stuff?' Adam wondered. 'The whole girl-scout bit?'

Harm looked at him. 'What, you don't get why a fifteen-year-old girl was sent to do a *man*'s work, that it?'

'No!' Adam protested. Then he shrugged. 'Well, maybe a bit.'

Abruptly, Harm left the path and started scaling the rugged hillside as easily as a spider would climb a wall. She reached a narrow rocky ledge and pulled herself up and onto it with a gymnast's grace. Then she pulled off a handful of plants, shoved them into the satchel she carried, and swiftly made the return journey. A little out of breath but with pride in her eyes, she looked at him. 'You get it now?'

Adam was impressed. 'I get it.'

He kept alert, looking all around as they climbed to higher ground. The sun was as hot as it was bright. The humid air carried no birdsong, and there was no breeze to stir the trees. There was no sign of life at all. As he and Harm pressed on into the jungle, he found himself flinching from pretty much every rustle and crack. But Harm only paused a few times before deciding it was safe to press on.

'How many raptors are on the island?' he whispered.

'Enough,' Harm said, studying scratch marks in a coconut tree. 'The island's about five kilometres square and there's maybe forty raptors in total.'

Adam blanched. 'As many as that?'

'Used to be more. But they kill each other.' She shrugged. 'Kind of like enemy tribes, I guess.'

Suddenly a grating whistle sounded from the long grass ahead of them. Adam froze, sweat prickling over his body, and looked to Harm. She held up a cautious hand to him, a mass of calluses. And then a huge bird burst out, easily two metres tall, its little head bobbing about at the end of a long, scrawny neck. Its body was a black, feathered oval with tail feathers speckling to grey and its long pink legs ended in two-pronged claws.

Adam let out a shaky breath. 'Is that an ostrich?'

'Uh-huh.' Harm nodded, holding back as the bird bobbed past. 'Kind of weird, huh? David says you only find them in Africa. So they must've been brought here with the dinosaurs.'

'There's lots of them?'

'Lots of one,' Harm answered, and seemed pleased at his puzzled face. 'See that white patch on the tail feathers? Every last one of these birds has an identical mark. David says they must've been grown from the same cells or something.'

'Clones,' breathed Adam. 'Geneflow must've put them out here as part of their experiment.'

'David's gonna love you.' Harm shook her head. 'Coming up with all these questions and theories.'

He gave a tentative smile. 'Question: can I have any more of that water?'

'Theory: you have a death-wish.'

If I have, thought Adam grimly, *I've been brought to the right place.*

They pressed on through the sun-spattered glades. Adam was grateful to the thick palms of the coconut trees for their shelter, even as the same questions buzzed uselessly through his head. *Where is my dad right now? Is Chen still alive? What is Geneflow trying to achieve?*

Why fill this island with dinosaurs?

'Wait here,' Harm told him quietly, selecting a coconut shell from the ground. She tapped it loudly, rapidly against a tree trunk. A high, hollow echo rang out, and was answered a few seconds later by an identical signal, sounding through the forest. 'All right, we're cool. Come on.'

Adam followed her with rising nerves to where a man and a woman stood wraith-like in the clearing. The man was lean and rangy, clothed in the ragged remains of jeans and a checked shirt. His dark beard was flecked with grey, and a denim sun hat sat on his head. At the sight of Adam he reached for a well-used machete at his waist.

'No, it's all right,' Harm told him quickly. 'Don't hurt him, he's about all I brought back with me.' She held up the bottle of water. 'Apart from this.'

The man lowered the machete and took the bottle from her almost reverently. 'Well done,' he murmured. He popped the cap and passed it to Lisa, who drank greedily. Just as quickly he pulled the bottle off her and took a smaller swig himself, sighing as he did so. Only then did he eye Adam. 'So . . . you're one of the survivors from the wreck.'

Adam nodded. 'You must be David?'

'David Wilder.'

'And you . . .' Adam turned to the woman, thin, blonde and hard-faced, and realized he'd seen her before. 'Lisa Brannigan?'

Lisa reacted as if waking from a dream. 'What? How would you know—'

'I've seen the video,' Adam told her. 'Loner got it to Jeremy Marrs at the Ethics place.'

'He did it.' Lisa ran over to Adam, who tried not to flinch from the smell of her. 'I never really believed he could . . . !'

'Adam knows about Geneflow too,' Harm added.

David came forward to join them, hope sparking

in his eyes. 'How many troops have they sent? Where are they?'

Lisa squeezed Adam's hand like a kid ready to cross the road. 'Are they going to get us out of here? Are they?'

Adam felt the weight of the survivors' stares. He looked nervously at Hturm, and she spoke for him. 'Adam here came with an FBI guy, weapons, and people to use them . . .' She took a deep breath. 'But he's the only one I've seen alive, and the guns could be anywhere.'

Adam watched as David's and Lisa's faces fell hard enough to bruise.

'So all we've really got,' David muttered at length, 'is another mouth to feed. A kid to look after.'

'I don't need looking after,' Adam shot back.

'Why would the FBI send a child anyway?' David pointed a finger at him. 'Are you telling us the truth?'

'My dad and I know about Geneflow's dinosaur experiments,' Adam informed him. 'They kidnapped us both in the summer, and . . .' He bit his tongue before he could add, *and now some crazy FBI agent's done the same thing.* He couldn't bring himself to stamp on these people's last hopes. 'Look, there's another ship out to sea,' Adam went on. 'My dad's on board with more men and more weapons, I bet. He'll be trying to get to me.'

'No ship can get past the sea creatures,' said David tersely. 'It's like they're trained to attack anything that comes too close. But . . . if the UN and the FBI are involved, they could send an airlift or something, right?'

'Yeah,' Adam said, smiling weakly. *Except the FBI man came on his own, and the UN have no idea what is happening right now.* 'We just have to hold tight.'

'Sorry, honey.' Lisa smiled uncertainly at Adam, touched his arm as if afraid he would disappear. 'It's not easy in this place. But I guess we can't stop hoping for miracles now.'

'We should search the area where Adam came ashore,' said Harmony. 'Other survivors might have weapons, or—'

She broke off as a whooshing, clattering noise carried through the forest. David and Lisa stood rigid.

'What is it?' Adam asked.

'Early warning,' Lisa muttered.

'Jungle vine tripwire, tied to a bundle of sticks,' David elaborated, crossing to a coconut tree and forming a stirrup with his hands. 'If the sticks fall over, we know we've got visitors.'

Harm stepped into his hands and propelled herself upward, hugging the trunk and climbing with the flats of her feet against the rough bark. Within seconds she had penetrated the thick palms that crowned the tree, their wide fleshy stalks supporting her weight. Seconds later she came down the trunk like a firefighter sliding down a pole, eyes wide and panic-stricken.

'Brutes?' whispered Lisa.

Harm shook her head. 'Two Vels, headed this way. One of them's holding something – metal and a bit of rope or something, couldn't see what.'

Lisa turned to David. 'What are they gonna do this time?'

'Come on.' David was white-faced as he turned and ran in the opposite direction. 'The dugout.'

Harm grabbed hold of Lisa's hand. Adam followed as they broke into a stumbling run through the fronds and bushes. 'What is this "dugout"?' he asked.

'Our only hiding place,' Harm told him.

'We sleep there most nights,' Lisa muttered. 'It's like being buried alive.'

Adam quickened his step, sweat soaking his body while his throat stayed sore and dry. He didn't think he'd ever felt thirstier in his life. He caught movement at ground level up ahead, shied away for a second. Then he realized it was David clearing grass away from a small hole dug out between the roots of a tree; the thick wooden gnarls forming a tough, narrow barrier to forcing the hole any wider. Beyond it lay a mass of branches heaped as if trying to conceal something.

'It's an old bunker,' said David as he worked. 'Built by American soldiers for jungle warfare against the Japanese in World War Two. Used to be bigger, but part of it caved in.'

Harm led Adam on but Lisa hung back. 'I hate it,' she was still muttering under her breath. 'Hate it, hate it.'

'Please.' David looked into her eyes, put his palms on the woman's shoulders. 'We're not losing anyone else. Right? No one else.'

Lisa lay down on her back, started wriggling through the hole feet first. David supported her by the arms as she squeezed through. Adam kept looking back into the trees, dreading the first glimpse of movement.

'Now you, Harm,' David said as Lisa's hair slipped from view. 'Help Adam through from the inside.'

Harm nodded. She pushed herself head first into the hole, gasping as she wormed her way through the gap.

David looked at Adam, a sheen of sweat on his face. The crashing through the trees was getting louder. 'Quickly.'

Adam got down on his back. He could barely fit both feet together through the hole. 'Is there room inside?'

'We'll make room. *Get in!*'

Bracing himself, Adam squeezed through the hole. Hands grabbed his flailing ankles, pulled hard to draw him down into the darkness. He had a panicked, suffocating moment as the hard-packed mud of the entrance dragged against his ears and hair. More hands pulled at his shirt and sides – and then he was dropping down into a dark, sweat-stinking concrete pit in the ground, pressed up against Harm and Lisa. Their bony limbs jabbed against his. The rasp of their breathing filled the stale air.

'Curl up,' Harm hissed at him. 'Make more space.'

With neat, economical movements, David worked himself into the tiny shelter, reached for something heavy at his feet and forced it with some difficulty up into the hole. The trickle of daylight was blocked off. Adam heard the scrape of concrete against earth as the makeshift plug was wedged securely into their point of entry, a metal pole holding it in place. Only a chink of sunlight broke through.

Adam held himself tensely in the pitch-darkness, trying not to shake. He was sure he could hear stamping noises getting closer. 'What happens now?'

'We wait for them to leave,' said David.

'But won't they sniff us out down here? I mean, their sense of smell must be—'

'That's enough,' David told him.

Adam turned to Lisa instead and lowered his voice further. 'Is that hole in the roof the only way in?'

'It is now,' Lisa muttered. 'A pack of Brutes stamped the roof in when they couldn't get through the main entrance. Most of the shelter collapsed.'

Adam swallowed hard. 'And you still use what's left?'

'What choice have we got?' Harm whispered.

The four fugitives heard grunts and heavy foot-falls. Then an earthy, scraping sound like a garden fork hitting concrete.

Lisa started to whimper as the plug in the ceiling began to budge, and a loud hissing sound started up, like someone using a spray can. Except the hissing went on. David held Lisa's hand. 'We're safe down here,' he breathed.

But then something poked down into sight through the narrow gap next to the concrete bung. Not rope. The end of a length of rubber hose. And immediately white smoke coiled out from inside.

'What is that?' Lisa held her hand to her mouth.

David started choking, gasping for breath. 'Gas,' he spluttered. 'Tear gas.'

'Gas?' Lisa wailed, incredulously. 'How did they—'

'Who cares how?' Adam's eyes felt suddenly on fire. 'We've got to block it!' He ripped at the hem of his shirt, trying to tear it free. But his efforts were hampered as the others started to jostle and push into the narrow space. Nose and eyes streaming, saliva coming so fast he thought he might hurl, Adam fell to his knees. Lisa was shrieking in his ear, David and Harm were coughing and retching as the gas misted over the crack of sunlight. The raptors above began to stamp their feet.

They're using human weapons against us, Adam realized, his throat on fire. *They're going to smash their way inside, and then reach in and pluck out our bodies.*

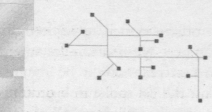

10: Stolen Prey

Adam could barely see, his eyes burning like someone had rubbed them with chilli peppers. He knocked against the base of the metal pole holding the concrete plug in place – just as a stamp from above smashed it in two. A chunk of rock hit his leg and sunlight burst in like a spotlight. Something metal clattered down into the tiny space – a canister, spewing out the evil smoke. Eyes awash, Adam saw a claw as big as his face plunge down into the dugout, grasping blindly. He grabbed the concrete and swung it at the creature's hand, trying to knock it away. But the claw closed around his wrist and with a choking gasp Adam found himself hauled up, clear out of the dugout.

Blazing sunlight hit his skin, closely followed by hard, scaly flesh. Before his terror could even fully register, he found himself thrown aside, winded on the ground, a tree root biting into his spine. He heard Lisa shriek and a deep, bestial snarl as the other Vel rooted about in the concrete cavity.

Forcing his swollen eyes apart he glimpsed through his tears a blurred red shape bearing down on him. Rank breath hissed into his face.

'You will join us,' the Vel spoke in a grating rasp as though choking up the syllables. 'All of you will join us for the feast.'

'No,' Adam moaned helplessly. 'No, please . . .' He felt his wrists being bound roughly and clumsily with the rubber tubing, cried out as the raptor's claws scraped at his flesh.

But then the monster was knocked clear by some massive impact. It grunted with pain as it slammed into something, started snarling and snapping its jaws. There was a wet crunch of flesh on flesh, a howl of anger. The foliage around Adam danced and shook as though alive and wild. A second roar, deeper and angrier, sounded to his left – the other Vel, close by. Whimpering with fear, Adam tried again to open his swollen eyes, but then the sounds of struggle broke off and something picked him up. Sharp claws pressed into the small of his back as it ran off, taking him away. Adam felt sharp, stubby feathers chafe his neck, his body clamped hard against folds of reptilian skin. *Another raptor*, he realized. *Got to be a Brute. Brutes hate Vels. It's stolen their prey.*

Harm's words in the boat ate through his scattered thoughts: *Killers.*

Helplessly, Adam began to struggle in the creature's grip. It was too strong. He couldn't overbalance it, and it didn't seem to feel the blows he rained down on its back. Any moment now he could imagine that acidic spray ejecting from its mouth, searing and softening his flesh . . .

But then suddenly he was dumped to the ground on his side. He lay for a few seconds, still choking and drooling from the gas. His eyes had cleared enough to see he was lying in long grass just beyond a leafy tangle of creepers. The space was wide open, no cover. Something was trampling quickly through the undergrowth towards him and there was nowhere to hide.

'Stay there,' came an eerie voice — a voice that made Adam picture the steam of breath on cold glass. And with a surge of sudden hope he realized it was a voice he'd heard before.

'Are . . .' He choked. 'Are you Loner? The one who helped Lisa? The one who—'

'Yes.' The voice was eerily soft. 'I am Loner.'

Adam blinked away his tears, focused — and then flinched. The blurred video he'd watched in the safety of a UN conference room had done no jus-tice at all to the scale and power of this creature before him. It stood taller than a man but hunched over in the classic prehistoric predator stance, arms hooked over and outstretched. Piercing orange eyes shone in the low, elongated head that crowned the thick curl of its neck. The scarlet-striped snout sniffed and quivered. Its thighs were bunched with corded muscle and the claws curving out from its hind feet were like butcher's hooks. A thicket of thorny quills blanketed its chest and shoulders.

The creature stood there, breathing heavily. Just watching. Impossible, but so real.

The stamping noise was getting louder. 'Is that the Vels?' Adam croaked.

'One of them. I killed the other.' Loner shifted his weight from foot to foot as though anxious or in distress. 'Stay where you are.'

'What?' Adam stared at him helplessly. 'But I've got to go, that raptor will see me, it'll—'

'Stay *still*. Trust me.'

Trust you? How can I? You're . . . Adam looked into Loner's unblinking eyes. *You're an impossible creature, put together by madmen from scraps of fossil, given powers no wild animal ever had . . .* He was scared and sickened but it was like some force was compelling him to keep searching out Loner's eyes. Then he found himself nodding. *If I'm wrong*, he thought, *I guess it won't hurt for very long.*

Loner turned abruptly and left the glade with a striding, bird-like gait, disappearing back into the thicker trees.

It was too late for Adam to move now in any

case. A raptor, similar in build to Loner only darker and with thicker stripes, burst from out of the foliage and skidded to a stop at the sight of the human prey before it. Hissing and snorting, it lowered its head and tore towards him, clawed feet kicking up the turf. Adam opened his mouth to scream.

But then, mid-charge, the creature dropped out of sight as it fell through the covering of foliage into a hidden pit beneath. *A trap*, Adam realized, his pulse rate as wild as the howling raptor in its prison of mud. *Loner must've dug the pit. I was the bait to lure that thing inside.*

He edged away nervously as the raptor began thrashing and clawing at the steep walls of the pit. But the next moment, the leafy vegetation to Adam's left exploded as Loner charged back out, built up speed and then jumped inside the narrow lane, his large feet trampling down on the raptor caught inside.

There was a wet, crunching sound, and a rattle of wheezing breath, and the captive raptor's struggles ceased.

Loner hauled himself back out from the pit, using the body lodged inside for leverage. Once clear, he lay on the ground, apparently exhausted.

Adam looked into the pale orange ovals of Loner's eyes; the sly intelligence of the predator shone there, as they had in the eyes of Zed. But here was something else too — uncertainty, maybe. Or regret.

'I had to,' Loner whispered.

'Uh . . .' Adam licked his dry lips. 'Had to what?'

'To kill.' Loner's breathing grew slower, more even. 'The first of my pack brothers I killed swiftly and by surprise. The second would have slashed my throat if I had not done this.' He stared down at the hole in the ground. 'I dug the pit for catching ostrich, you see? There were spikes at the bottom. But . . . not sharp enough.'

Adam shuddered. 'So you jumped on that thing to . . . to push it down onto the spikes?'

'Not "that thing",' Loner snapped. 'Pack brother.' His tail flicked over the edges of the pit as if to caress the mangled remains inside. 'He was like me. But not like me.' He looked at Adam and edged closer. 'Same with you. You are like Harmony, David, Lisa . . . but not.'

'I . . . I just got here. Is that what you mean?' Still hugging himself, Adam looked away. The weird reality of his situation was sinking in. *I'm having a full-on conversation with a dinosaur.* He'd grown used to Zed grunting syllables at him like a belligerent child. But Loner spoke more like Adam himself. *Geneflow's techniques have grown way, way more advanced — and in just a few months.*

Adam felt more afraid than ever.

'I saw you on the beach.' Loner rose up slowly on his haunches. 'Smelled you. I was following you, when my pack brothers . . .' He blinked. 'How do I know you so deep down? How do I know . . . the *thought* of you?'

Adam flinched as the bestial head pushed slowly towards him on the elongating S of its neck. 'You . . .' He swallowed hard. 'I guess you were taught with something called Think-Send. My dad invented it, and he used my brainwaves to get the whole thing working.'

'Like an echo in my head,' Loner said hoarsely. 'Yes?'

'Maybe . . .' Adam could see every scale of that rough, reptilian face now, close enough to touch, and thought of Zed. 'Maybe there's a trace of my thoughts in your head. It happened that way before. I'm Adam Adlar.'

'Adlar . . .' The towering creature nudged Adam's head, scraping its scales against his skin. Adam closed his eyes, held his breath. He realized that Loner was doing the same. Then they both released a shaky sigh at the same time, and the raptor recoiled. Adam, with relief, fell backwards, supporting himself with his hands. He felt like a lion tamer who'd just put his head in the lion's mouth on the first day of the job.

A fresh crashing started up from the jungle, but from the choking and slow speed Adam realized it was Harm and the others. 'Hello?' he called to them.

'Adam?' David called back. 'Thank God!' The crashing got faster and louder, and David was first to emerge from the trees, his haggard face streaked with tears. He was leading Lisa by the hand, whose eyes were swollen and closed. Harm was last out, looking sick and scared. She saw Loner hunched there on the ground and reacted, crying out.

'It is me, Harmony.' The raptor turned and lowered his head, almost as if bowing. 'Do not be afraid.'

'We thought you must be dead, Loner.' David pulled off his hat and wiped his glistening brow, trying to stifle his coughing. 'We haven't seen you for so long.'

'I have been in hiding,' he said quietly, rocking on his haunches. 'Fresh-caught human prisoners at the Vel camp saw me there and begged me to help them as before. My rulers now know that I have sided with your kind. They tried to kill me.' Loner bowed his head. 'Like you . . . I am a fugitive now.'

'Well . . . Thank you.' David surveyed the pit's grisly contents. 'You saved our lives.'

He's talking to a dinosaur as casually as . . . Adam caught himself. *As casually as I would.* When confronted with the reality of talking dinosaurs, you could either crack up or get to grips with it. How long had he wished to talk about his experiences to people who wouldn't laugh in his face, who would understand?

Yay, he thought bitterly. *Let's hunker down in the blood-stained grass for a cosy chat.*

Lisa's fingers strayed to her puffy eyes. 'What was that stuff they used on us?'

'From the way our mucous glands have been affected, some sort of tear gas, I think.' David pulled a rusted canister from his shorts' pocket. 'Probably World War Two issue. The Vel camp is an old military base, after all, and we know they've found leftover munitions.'

'Like the explosives they set off on the old airstrip.' Lisa shuddered. 'Testing out human weapons.'

Adam looked at David. 'Did you used to teach history?'

'Science.' David scrutinized the canister. 'Lucky for us it must have lost some of its potency over the years. In that enclosed space it could have suffocated us.'

'How come it didn't hurt them?' Harm wondered.

'Geneflow probably bred them with better lungs than us,' said Adam.

'My throat's burning,' Lisa said, tears squeezing from her swollen lids. 'Evil monsters. They're not happy just to hunt us now, they're trying to torture us.'

Loner looked to be getting agitated. 'We must all leave here. My brothers will soon be missed. More will come. The Council of Blood has spoken – all humans are to be gathered.'

Adam shook his head. 'For this feast of theirs?'

'Then we're finished.' Harm coughed noisily, rubbing at her neck. 'The Vels can sniff us out wherever we are.'

'They've been picking off groups like ours one by one for so long,' said David. 'Why the sudden urgency to get us?'

'Uh . . .' Adam got awkwardly to his feet. 'Isn't the question more why's it taken the raptors so long? You've been here three months – surely they could've hunted you down easily.'

Harm shot him a look. 'Enough of them have tried.'

But David was shaking his head. 'It's not that simple, Harm. Adam's right. The fact we've survived all this time can't only be down to luck, or caution, or skill. For the most part, the raptors have been content to feed on the ostriches Geneflow brought here. And by the way, ostriches are the perfect animals for this environment, you know that? Because they don't need to drink water. Some they make themselves, the rest they get out of vegetation – so they don't compete with the raptors *or* us.'

'School's out, Mr Wilder, 'K? We don't need a lesson.' Harm crossed her arms, but her surly tone couldn't disguise the worry on her face. 'What are you saying?'

Irritation flared in his reddened eyes. 'I'm saying what we already know – that this place has been set up for some kind of an experiment.' David looked round gravely at his audience. 'Only I don't think it's just about the dinosaurs. Us humans are a part of the experiment too.'

'And all humans must be gathered,' Loner said in his icy whisper. 'For the feast.'

Adam felt a shiver trail down his back as the penny dropped. 'Even if we manage to stop the raptors putting us on their menu – when the experiment ends . . . what happens then?'

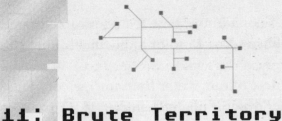

11: Brute Territory

Adam's words hung heavily in the air for a few moments. Then Harm's next coughing fit, loud and hacking, kicked them to the tropical kerbside.

'This conversation is real fun,' she said weakly, 'but I've got to have some water. My throat feels like it's been peeled raw.'

David nodded slowly as if summoning the strength to continue. 'We need to bathe your eyes too, Lisa,' he said. 'You've had some sort of allergic reaction.'

Lisa nodded. 'The water bottle from the boat—?'

David shook his head. 'It split when we were stamping round inside the dugout. Nothing left.'

'Nothing left,' Lisa echoed, and seemed to deflate. 'I hardly tasted it.'

'What else do you do for drinking water?' Adam asked. 'I mean, with so many raptors here . . .'

'Loner and his friends can drink the sea water,'

David said. 'I don't know how. It ought to kill them. They must have some kind of high-functioning salt gland . . .'

'We get most of our water from unripe coconuts,' said Lisa, her voice dull and distant. 'And most of our food from the ripe ones.'

'Forgot to say,' Harm mumbled, pulling the handful of plants from her satchel, 'I got us some purslane.' She pressed it into Lisa's palm, and the woman shoved it into her mouth, chewing quickly. Harm offered some to David but he passed his share straight to Lisa. She took it willingly, muttering thanks.

Loner tapped his tail on the ground, almost as though shyly knocking to enter the conversation. 'I can collect water for you,' he said in his soft, cold voice, 'from the rain-traps in the north cliffs.'

'We haven't been back that way for weeks,' Harm realized.

'Too far to trek in our condition,' David reminded her. 'We'd use up more energy than we'd get back.'

'I can collect the water,' Loner repeated. 'And food too.'

Adam regarded the raptor. 'Thank you,' he said.

Loner turned his eyes to Adam. 'I will need help to carry it back.'

'I'll go,' Adam volunteered.

'You just got here,' Harm retorted. 'And already

you've needed your butt saving twice.'

Adam smarted at the criticism. 'I've ridden a flying mutant dinosaur across the Atlantic, OK? I got kidnapped by Geneflow but I got out again. I even smacked Samantha Josephs.' He felt himself redden, embarrassed at his outburst. 'I can handle myself.'

Loner's gaze grew more intense. 'You have met Josephs before?'

'That's kind of why I was brought here,' Adam admitted.

'That and to fetch and carry food and drink for us,' said Harm drily. 'Loner, can I come too? Two can carry more.'

The raptor's cold eyes turned to the teacher. 'If David agrees?'

'I can't go,' said David. 'Lisa's too vulnerable to leave with her eyes like this.' He sighed. 'Just be careful. All of you.'

'How do we get to these cliffs?' asked Adam, eyeing the muscles bunching under Loner's scaly hide and rubbing his own bruised ribs.

'I cannot fly,' Loner said, bowing his head as if in apology, 'but it will be fastest if I can carry you both on my back, at least some of the way.'

Nervously, Adam clambered onto the raptor's ridged, striped back. He didn't want to hold on too tight. The sight of Loner leaping into the pit and trampling his brother into the spikes flashed into his head.

'Guess this won't mean much to you, Adam, if you're used to travelling this way.' Harm climbed on behind him. 'As for me, I don't think I could ever get used to it.'

Adam was going to protest when Loner lurched forwards. He grabbed hold of the raptor's neck and Harm held onto his waist, squeezing so hard he had a job to breathe. Then they were away, clattering into the jungle and picking up speed, each footfall jarring through Adam's bones. He held on tighter, feeling hard, reptilian flesh eating into his arms. His heart whacked wildly as they thudded on through the jungle at incredible speed, vines and vegetation whipping at them. Adam had no idea how fast they were going. He shut his eyes and clung on.

Adam threw his head back to Harm. 'What if we run straight into more raptors?'

'Their scents will tell me when I am close,' Loner hissed.

Harm smiled tightly. 'He can hear and run at the same time. What d'you call that – Z-multi-tasking?'

Adam didn't bother to answer, concentrating on holding on. Loner's endurance was incredible – if anything he was picking up the pace as they left the overgrown forest and climbed a hillside, building and building speed until he reached the top and leaped over the rise. Adam cried out, first in terror, then exhilaration as they landed safely on the other side of the hill. He began to laugh and found he couldn't stop, laughing so hard it felt almost like crying as the tension and fear jerked out of him.

He looked down. The blue sea fringed the beach way below to their left. It all looked so beautiful from up here; Adam could hardly reconcile the tranquillity with the horror and violence he'd lived through. He raised his eyes, stared at the horizon. There was no sign of the *Pahalu*, but he went right on staring.

'Looking for your dad's boat?' Harm murmured in his ear.

Adam sighed and nodded. 'It is out there, Harm. There were guys guarding my dad, friends of Agent Chen.'

'The FBI man?' Harm queried.

'Right.' Adam nodded. 'And those guys wouldn't run out on Chen any more than Dad would run out on me. They'll be looking for a way to get here.' He half-expected Harm to make some sneery comment. But she just held on to his waist a little more tightly as Loner kept on ploughing on through the wild landscape.

Adam had no idea how much time had passed, but his spine was starting to feel like jelly. Loner finally slowed as they reached a wide sweep of sandy rock half smothered in green tangles. His breath was coming in short, rough snatches, and his tongue was hanging from the side of his jaws like a thirsty dog.

'Thank you,' Adam said awkwardly.

Harm scrambled off the raptor's back. As she did so she almost overbalanced. Adam reached out a hand automatically, but the raptor's tail moved faster, curling round Harm's waist to catch her.

'I have you,' Loner murmured, helping her to steady herself.

Adam concentrated on keeping upright himself as he swung his legs stiffly down to the ground, his muscles tensed and trembling.

'We must not be long,' Loner said quietly, falling heavily to the ground, keeping low. 'Brutes have passed this way, not long since.'

'David didn't think they could climb so far.' Harm looked troubled. 'The cliffs overlook their camp, but the other side is a sheer drop. Why would they travel all the way to the other side and round here?'

Adam froze. 'We're on top of their camp?'

'No such thing as a safe place on this island,'

Harm told him. 'Loner, is it safe to check them out, see what they're doing?'

'Your scent will blow back this way,' Loner told her. 'But be quick.'

Harm was already climbing up the sandy slope of the cliff, picking a deliberate path through gaps in the spiky foliage. Adam followed her, grateful for his trainers, joining her at the top of the rise. Cautiously he peered over the rocky precipice.

It was like looking down on a real-life horror movie.

His skin crawled as he saw that dozens of Brutes had colonized a sheltered inlet. The sand, once white, was now stained with crimson shadows. One Brute, larger than the others, was picking over a large pile of what could only be bodies. With horror, Adam recognized a pile of bloody rags as clothes torn from the drowned men he'd pulled out of the sea.

'They've been building up their larder,' Harm whispered. 'That big one, she's like, their queen.'

'Queen?'

'The females are tougher than the males.'

Adam noticed a kind of coronet of barbed wire tangled round the queen's head. He stared trans-fixed as she bit greedily into the pile, holding the hunks of meat in her powerful arms. Most she swall-owed but some she spat out onto the sand. Other

Brutes hung back, watching intently and competing for the scraps, the largest roaring and spraying acid at smaller rivals who came too close, maintaining the pecking order.

'Every Brute for himself,' Harm murmured.

Feeling sick, Adam looked further along the shore. He noticed that some driftwood and a number of large sails had been turned into a makeshift shelter of some kind with boulders blocking the entrance.

'Is that the queen's private chambers?' wondered Adam.

'I don't know,' said Harm. 'It wasn't there the last time I passed this way.'

Adam shuddered to think what the shelter might contain. It creeped him out, the way these creatures could plan and build; it was almost as scary as the way they could speak.

And kill.

'Seen enough?' Harm murmured. 'We've got stuff to do.'

She started to retreat back down the rise towards Loner, and Adam followed. But then he heard a disturbance in the foliage in the valley below. His heart seemed to stop as he looked down, fearing discovery. Harmony had frozen too. But it was only an ostrich, bursting from the tree line, running spooked—

And straight into the path of a Brute. The creature had been hiding itself in the long grass. Now it reared up and spat acid. The ostrich weaved, turned and bolted back towards the tree line. Before it could get there, a second, larger Brute – a real monster with one eye missing and scarred over – darted out of hiding and grabbed it in its jaws. With a flick of its great grey neck it jerked the bird off the ground and slammed it against a tree, snapping its neck.

Adam held very, very still. *If I can see them, they can see me.*

The one-eyed killer held the large bird above its grey, scarred head and roared. The other Brute bobbed its head lower as it approached, holding out its claws behind it – gestures of submission. Only then did One-Eye tear off a wing and a leg from its catch and throw them to the ground, devouring the rest itself. The other greedily ate its lesser spoils, and followed One-Eye back into the tree line. One-Eye paused for a moment, scenting the air. It turned and seemed to look in Adam's direction. Then it snapped its jaws, turned again and vanished from sight.

Adam breathed a shaky sigh of relief.

'Bad boys,' Harm breathed. 'Hunting for themselves and not taking it back to their queen.'

'The smaller one was female,' said Loner.

He'd stolen up behind them so quietly Adam hadn't even noticed. 'She is weaker than most. He is injured.'

'Do they come hunting by themselves 'cause they can't compete with the others?' Adam wondered.

Loner nodded. 'Dangerous. Their ruler punishes with death.'

'Figures,' said Adam.

'C'mon, let's do what we came here for.' Harm began searching a patch of land nearby. Carefully she pulled away a thin layer of dead grass to reveal a length of clear plastic sheeting.

It had been stretched flat over a shallow conical pit in the sand. A rock sat on top, placed carefully in the middle. Harm lifted the stone aside, and Adam scrambled down to watch as she carefully turned over the transparent sheet to reveal three coconut shells split in half, nestling in the sand beneath. Each was half-full with water.

'Wow,' Adam said. 'Neat trick.'

'The plastic washed up on the shore one time. Must've come from one of the wrecks.' Harm lifted one of the half-shells. 'So, anyways, you lay it over this hole in the sand, and the sun warms the sand beneath and takes out the moisture. The moisture cools on the plastic, turns to water and drips into the cups.' She gave him a weary smile. 'Great to be cast away with a science teacher, huh? If only he weren't such a pain in the ass.'

'He is?'

'He's a teacher isn't he?' She leaned forward over the crumpled plastic sheet, where a few more droplets had collected. In a sudden darting movement, she lowered her face and lapped at it in sudden desperation. Adam watched, uncomfortable. Then Harm glanced back at him.

'Sorry,' she whispered. 'Should've shared.'

She continued to lean forward, reaching underneath a bush and pulling out an ancient empty carton of Sunny D. 'Here,' she said. 'Pour the water into there for carrying. I don't trust myself right now.' She straightened up. 'I'll fetch coconuts so we can stoke our supplies a little, 'K?'

'Right.' Adam watched her cross to a towering palm tree and climb it with practised ease. Then he took each hollowed-out shell and poured the water carefully.

'Adam.' Loner's voice carried from the base of the rise. 'I think I know why Brutes came up here. I found these.'

Turning, Adam saw the raptor was holding something in his hands. His insides lurched as he realized it was a pair of binoculars. He recognized them – they were Chen's. The man had been using them last night.

'The Brutes must've picked these up from the beach,' Adam said, tugging them gently free from Loner's claws. 'They belong to an FBI agent.'

Loner stared at him. 'A what?'

'Sorry. I mean, a kind of policeman. From America.'

'And this agent . . .' An edge of urgency had stolen into Loner's voice. 'He came from this ship you say is out there?'

'Yes, but I don't know if he made it here alive or not. If they've got his binoculars it could mean . . .' Adam remembered Brad's burning face on the beach and shook his head wearily. 'Why would Brutes need binoculars anyway?'

Loner pointed into the distance, to where a concrete building could be seen between two hilltops. 'The Vel camp,' he said. 'The Brutes have been spying on the Vels.'

Adam studied the scratched binoculars and saw the 'day' setting had already been selected. *Brutes aren't so stupid*, he reminded himself, as he placed the bins to his eyes and looked for himself. The magnification was impressive. He could see the cracks and crumbles in the concrete, and sheets of corrugated iron blocking up a doorway. In front of it, two Vels were standing guard beside a kind of scrap barricade — splintered desks, an old refrigerator, chunks of concrete, the rusted chassis of an ancient motorbike, with thick chains snaking between the component parts.

'They look like they're expecting an attack,' said Adam. 'Is it you they're worried about?'

Loner shook his head. 'How can I be a threat to them? I was one of the sick ones for many weeks.'

Adam looked at him. 'Sick?'

'When my young days ended, my mind . . . changed. I felt hot. Weak.' His lips curled awkwardly around the word. 'I saw things that could not be real. There were flashes in my sight. I felt things in my mind I did not understand.' He breathed out sharply, spittle flecking the corners of his mouth. 'There were others like me. The councillors keep sick ones strapped down in a dark room. They told us we were just like them. They told us we should *act* like them.' Loner shook that huge striped head. 'But I knew I was not like them. I had a name. They beat me and bled me but I would not let go of who I am . . .'

Adam could just imagine a raptor doctor's bedside manner. *Loner's like Zed*, he thought. *He's learned to think for himself.* He stared long and hard into the animal's deep orange eyes. 'So what happened?'

'In the dark room, at night when it was quiet, I saw *people*. Human people who came out of the wall . . . in special clothes to protect them.'

'And you weren't crazy, were you,' breathed

Adam. 'The people came from Geneflow, right?'

'They scraped scabs from our wounds. Put wires in our blood.' Loner shook slightly as he spoke. 'Fixed metal against our heads. I thought they were dreams . . . until I saw them press numbers on a pad to make the wall open and close.' He blinked at Adam. 'One night I pressed the numbers too. The dark room opened onto light.'

'That's how you found out that this place was part of an experiment,' Adam realized.

'They did not know I could get into their base,' said Loner, his claws twitching. 'I was smart. I got out lots. I got further each time. Into rooms. Down stairs. I listened to Josephs. I watched and . . . learned.'

'There must be real proof of what they're doing inside that base, if we could just get to it . . .' Adam looked out to sea again, longing to spy a ship on the horizon. 'How many people does Josephs have here?'

'Not many, I think,' said Loner. 'But they have no scent. They are hard to find.'

Adam nodded. 'Geneflow has this sort of anti-stink spray. Helps them stay hidden from their creations.'

'They came to the dark room lots,' Loner remembered. 'But more Vels turned sick. In time, the councillors said they would not waste more food on us. They took us away from camp and left us to hunt for ourselves.' Loner looked out to sea just as Adam had. 'Most died. They starved or were killed by Brutes. Only I survived. I don't think I was truly sick. My mind grew clearer.' His head snapped back round, voice growing fiercer as he bore down on Adam. 'And I knew what I had to do. Stop all this. Stop Geneflow. But the councillors would not listen, could not understand. They hate me, fear me. Because I am different.'

Adam shrank back a little. 'Didn't you show your . . . your pack the door in the wall? Tell them that they were part of an experiment?'

'I said, Adam, they would not listen. The old sick room had been made a forbidden place in case sickness spread. No one would go there.' Agitated, Loner rocked back and forth as if getting ready to spring. 'But even if they had listened to me . . . even if we had killed Josephs' humans . . . Geneflow would send more humans to kill all of us.' He shook his large, serpentine head. 'Nowhere to run to on this island. No escape.'

'I get you.' It was all Adam could do not to bolt for his life but he forced himself to stand his ground. 'So you had to get help from the outside world. You made the message.'

He looked at Adam almost accusingly. 'I risked my life, creeping inside Geneflow's base to send it.'

'And it worked,' Adam said quickly, holding up the binoculars. 'It was worth it, right? Help's come.'

'It has not worked well enough,' Loner hissed. 'Not yet. And time is running out.'

'If only we could get another message to Doctor Marrs,' said Adam shakily. 'Warn him about the underwater guard dogs. If he could deal with them so proper troops could land here . . .'

Loner snorted and sank back to his haunches. 'We would never get as far as the sick room. My brothers and sisters would tear us apart.'

'Hey.' Harm was approaching with an armful of shiny green fruits. 'Guess we should be getting back with the water for the others.'

At once, Loner seemed to forget his frustration, turning to her and bowing his head. Harm eyed him warily and held out some coconuts for Adam to take while she adjusted her bulging satchel. He dropped one as he tried to carry them all, but Loner scooped it up and scraped the top against the sickle-like claw on his right leg. It sliced through the hard fruit's tough skin like a knife opening a hard-boiled egg.

'Drink,' Loner said softly, holding out the fruit to Harm and Adam and looking back out to sea. 'You are going to need your strength.'

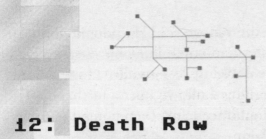

12: Death Row

The journey back to David and Lisa was more exhausting and painful than exhilarating. Still perched precariously on Loner's back, Adam's fingers and palms were covered in cuts from the raptor's sharp, stubby feathers and his stomach muscles had been clamped hard for so long his guts felt lined with broken glass. They'd had to take a longer route to the dugout to avoid a pack of Brutes, hunting in the brush and jungle.

'Thank God.' David jumped up as Loner came loping into the clearing and dropped to his knees, allowing Adam and Harm to scramble off. 'I thought you were never coming.' He snatched the carton from Adam, then saw the binoculars sticking out of his jeans pocket. 'Where'd you find those?'

'They were Agent Chen's.' Adam briefly explained how and where Loner had found them.

'Seems we have something to thank your FBI friend for at least,' said David. 'Anything that helps us keep tabs on the raptors . . .' He poured about a capful of the water and carefully dabbed it on Lisa's eyes. They were looking less swollen now, Adam was glad to note. David allowed her a further capful of the precious liquid to drink, then poured another for Harm and Adam.

Loner broke open more coconuts, ripe and unripe, and the ragged party ate and drank greedily in silence. The milk tasted unbelievably gross and sour to Adam and he found himself longing for burgers and chips and an ice-cold Coke.

David must've noticed his expression. 'Don't waste a drop,' he warned. 'That coconut water's chock full of nutrients.'

'When we die,' Harm muttered, 'we'll be in amazing shape.'

As Adam gouged the last white flesh from a coconut husk he heard distant animal cries and groans.

Lisa stiffened. 'Sounds like Brutes.'

'Something's got them stirred up,' David agreed.

Harm looked between the pit and Loner. 'D'you think they can smell those two Vels you offed?'

Loner was staring as flies buzzed over the corpse of his pack brother in the pit, as if tracking their intricate movements. 'This place will not be safe much longer,' he said at last. 'Vels will be coming here to gather you.'

'For the feast,' Adam murmured.

'Where can we go?' The way Lisa said the words it wasn't so much a question as a sigh of despair.

'Is there nowhere on the island that will give us cover?' Adam asked.

'The Vel camp would give us plenty,' said Harm sarcastically. 'And if we ask real nicely, maybe this Josephs woman will let us use her phone to charter a jet out of here.'

'I just asked,' Adam shot back.

'There's a derelict supply store at the airstrip,' David reflected. 'But there's too much open ground around there, no cover. If the raptors sniffed us out we wouldn't stand a chance . . .'

Adam turned to Loner who was hanging back, his orange eyes taking in everything. 'Hey,' he realized guiltily. 'You haven't eaten anything.'

'I dug another trap for ostrich,' said Loner slowly. 'Perhaps for now you can hide there.' He paused. 'It is near the bone pit.'

Harm shook her head. 'We can't.'

'The smell of the dead is strong around the pit,' Loner went on. 'It would help . . . to mask your living smell.'

Lisa looked almost pleadingly at David. 'I hate it there. Hate it.'

'You think I don't?' David looked grim. 'This is about survival.'

'What *is* the bone pit?' Adam looked between them, unease growing.

'A mass grave,' said Lisa, her red swollen eyes lending violence to her stare, her voice heavy as stone. 'Human bones piled high as a hill.'

Adam took a shaky breath. 'The wreck survivors who were killed here on the island?'

Harm shook her head, not meeting his eyes.

'When we hatched,' said Loner, 'we had no parents to provide for us . . . We did not understand anything but hunger. Hunger, and how to stop it.'

'The hatchlings needed a large food source to sustain them until they were old enough to hunt,' David confirmed. 'So they glutted themselves on the nearest meal.' He lowered his voice. 'Hundreds of people taken to this island and killed.'

'People were brought here to be raptor food?' said Adam. 'No way.'

'It is true,' Loner said, a dark shine in his eyes. 'Now we must go. The Brutes are getting closer.'

'Loner's right,' David muttered, as Harm took Lisa's hand and helped her to stand. 'We'll talk as we move.'

Adam wasn't sure how long they journeyed through the jungle. Time could be judged only by the slow climb of the sun across the sky, its light clawing its way feebly through the thick canopy of leaves. It was a humid, shadowy world. Silence reigned here; a silence so thick it begged to be broken. Adam imagined the dragon-hawk head of a Brute swooping down from behind to bite through his neck . . .

No, he thought, trying to calm himself. *Loner would warn us.* The crimson-dark raptor led the way, moving quietly with his curious, birdlike gait. Harm and Lisa walked just behind him, while Adam and David took up the rear. Adam's nostrils began to twitch at a soft, sickly-sweet, rotten smell. The more they walked, the worse it became. His stomach began to turn.

'It's up ahead,' David murmured. Harm and Lisa held hands as they stepped through into a sunny clearing.

Following them out, Adam found that a bare, circular area had been carved from a jungle hillside, the sides sloping down sharply and muddily into an oval pit of churned and stinking earth. And there, cracked and trampled in the mud, were the bones. A carpet of skulls and ribcages, femurs and thighbones and who knew what, some still wrapped in scraps of orange fabric.

Loner held back from the ragged group. 'I will make my ostrich trap bigger. Big enough to hold four,' he said quietly. 'It is close by.' With that he skirted round the pit and disappeared into the leafy shadows across the clearing.

Adam slumped back against a tree, his legs trembling, nausea and anger sending his heart into a driving thump. 'Why?' he murmured. 'Why would Geneflow go to the trouble of bringing people here to feed the raptors when they had the cloned ostriches?'

Lisa turned to him. 'Isn't it obvious? They wanted to give their raptors a taste for human meat right from the start.' Her face twisted in a sneer. 'When Geneflow are through with whatever it is they're doing, they'll let these raptors out into the world so they can eat everyone.'

'It can't be that,' David said gently, taking hold of her arm. 'If that were true, why release the ostriches onto the island for them to eat? And why are the Vels keeping people prisoner—?'

Lisa shook off his hand. 'All right, if you've got all the answers, why'd they do it? *Why'd they feed these things the people we loved?*'

Adam felt a cold prickling down his back. 'What?'

She jabbed a finger at the bones. 'My husband wound up in that pit. My Andy . . . just a pile of picked-clean bones.'

'But . . .' Adam wasn't sure if he should push this but had to know. 'I, uh, thought your husband was executed . . . back in September?'

Lisa stared at him blankly. 'What?'

'That's what Agent Chen said, that your husband was given a lethal injection—'

'Andy died here. We found the name badge from his prison uniform.' She pulled out a scrap of white fabric from her pocket, where BRANNIGAN, A was printed in black capitals. Then she unfolded it to reveal a little band of gold inside. 'His wedding ring. I put that on his finger and I took it from a . . . a half-chewed bone . . .'

Harm put her arm around Lisa as she began to sob in silence, and turned from the bone pit, eyes dull. 'What's left of my dad must be in there some-where too.'

Adam didn't understand. 'But . . . I thought you said you were flying out to visit your dad when you had to land here?' He turned to David. 'You were on board that plane too, right? Where was it really going?'

'It was taking us to see family.' David pushed out a long breath. 'Relatives who'd gotten off death row. Killers, given a second chance . . .' He wiped his eyes, gave a bitter laugh. 'They had no idea what they were really saying yes to.'

'But Agent Chen showed me the report,' Adam protested, lowering his voice. 'Lisa's husband *was* executed a few months back.'

'A cover-up,' said David. 'I'll bet you'd find a similar report on Harm's father, my sister . . . on everyone who wound up here.' He wiped his nose crossly on his wrist. 'They were told they would take part in a top-secret experimental prison pro- gramme – the Alta-Vita process, designed to rehabilitate even the most hardened criminals.'

'Alta-Vita?' Adam nodded. 'That's the name of one of Geneflow's projects.'

David ignored him, staring into space. 'The programme was designed to give them a better appreciation of what it means to be human. If they responded well they'd be eligible for parole. And if they didn't, their sentences would be reduced to life imprisonment just for taking part.'

'So, nothing to lose,' said Adam. 'But surely the prison governors wouldn't just hand criminals over . . .'

'They helped select candidates and handled everything in top secret to avoid an outcry from the victims' families,' David went on. 'They must have been fed a good line. Imagine if we *could* turn death row offenders into model citizens . . .'

Instead they were turned into raptor food. Adam pulled his top up over his nose to try and lessen the stench. 'I still don't see why they didn't take people it's less easy to track, like homeless people, run- aways, missing persons. Wouldn't that be easier than dealing with the prison staff and fobbing off the victims' families and—?'

He never finished his argument. A sudden, swelling sound like building thunder shook through the clearing, and the next moment two towering, rangy Brutes came crashing out of the foliage just a few metres from where they were standing.

'Soft-skins,' crooned one, slightly smaller but meaner-looking. '*Other* soft-skins.' The way its huge jaws mangled familiar words reminded him of Zed, only more savage and hate-filled.

The larger of the two raptors nodded. It had only one eye, and Adam suddenly realized that these were the animals he and Harm had watched from the north cliffs – the two who'd flouted their queen's laws by hunting and eating alone. He remembered the way one had spat at the ostrich to drive it into the jaws of the other.

They'll do the same to us, he thought numbly.

'Where are the others, soft-skins?' One-Eye was staring at David and Adam, his tail like a giant scorpion's, flexing over his shoulder. 'Where?'

The female Brute started stomping towards them, blood and acid drooling from her jaws. Even she was a good head taller than Loner. Adam was about to run for his life when the vegetation beside the Brute crashed apart as Loner reappeared, head lowered, charging at high speed.

The clearing erupted in wholesale carnage.

'You?' the female barked – as Loner's head

crunched into her side like a scaly cannonball and the momentum sent them plunging into the bone pit in an explosion of ivory. For a few seconds the fight was a chaotic clatter of bones and flashing claws as both raptors struggled to snare a sure footing.

David jerked into life, dragging Lisa and Harm away from the edge of the pit just as Loner struggled to his feet and drove both sets of powerful talons down into his opponent's chest, shattering quills and splitting flesh.

'Behind you, Loner!' Adam yelled, as One-Eye lumbered towards him.

Loner used the body of the smaller Brute as a springboard, leaping across to solid ground at the pit's edge. But One-Eye lunged with claws outstretched and landed a powerful blow against Loner's throat.

Adam closed his eyes for a moment as blood ran from the wound. But Loner stayed standing, staggering aside just as One-Eye spat mouth-acid at his face in a long arc. Lisa shrieked with pain as the juices splashed her bare legs instead. She convulsed and fell against a tree.

David put his arms around her, hauling her away from the struggling animals, terrified. 'I've got you,' he whispered.

Adam stared, paralysed with fear as the attacking Brute swung its club-like tail into Loner's legs. The Vel rolled backwards, his tail striking Harm in the stomach. She fell like a ninepin, crying out as she cracked the back of her head on a sun-bleached skull baked into the mud. Adam tried to emulate David and drag her away. The human skull grinned blankly at his desperate efforts. Another jet of acid sprayed the earth beside him. He saw Loner was locked in a bloody bearhug with One-Eye, the tough scales on his face oozing yellow and blistering, barking in pain and anger as he drove his attacker back into the undergrowth on the far side of the pit, his claws clamping its jaws shut. But the bloodied female Brute had risen like a grisly spectre from the bone pit and now stamped after Loner, clearly set on revenge . . .

And then he heard David and Lisa yell out in terror. Turning, Adam found that yet another Brute had appeared behind them, its face scuffed and scarred, blocking any escape the way they had come. Its dark eyes were hate-filled slits and its crooked teeth dripped acid as the jaws widened.

Trapped, thought Adam. *This time there's no way out.*

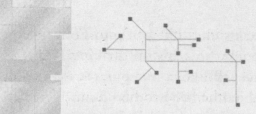

13: Killing Time

A loud, thundering boom cracked out from somewhere behind Scuffed-Face. The monster lurched forward, claws outstretched for David's neck. But the teacher threw himself to the ground, taking Lisa with him. Both rolled aside as, with another explosion of noise from the undergrowth, the Brute jerked and pitched forward, face down onto the ground.

Still crouched over Harm's prone body, Adam stared at a purple welt on the back of Scuffed-Face's skull. *That sounded like . . . gunshots?*

A man with oriental features pushed into sight from the dark green shadows. He was dirty, sweat-soaked, with a big pack on his back – and wielding a massive shotgun.

On his knees, David stared. 'Who the—?'

'Agent Chen!' Adam rose, sheer relief washing through him to see a familiar face. 'Are you—?'

'Not now, kid.' Chen helped up Lisa and then turned back to the thick jungle. 'Doc? Doc, come on, man!' He took aim with the shotgun as further crashing came from the bushes – then lowered it as Dr Stone from the *Hula Queen* staggered into sight, clutching an old leather bag to his chest.

Adam felt a weird surge of relief and anger to see again the man who'd kept him tranquillized for so many days. Stone's grey hair was soaked with sweat, he was gasping for breath and his face was badly cut. A fourth Brute loomed out of the undergrowth behind the doctor and Chen opened fire. The giant raptor's head jerked as the shot cracked into its skull, and it roared in anger.

'Ten-gauge shot barely breaks the skin,' Chen muttered, blasting the Brute a second time, sending it reeling out of sight.

'There're two more Brutes back there,' Adam said, pointing in the direction of Loner's headlong charge. Then he saw that Dr Stone was leaning heavily against a tree, clutching his chest. 'You OK?'

Stone nodded briefly, as Chen turned to the speechless David. 'There's more of those things on our tail. Get Adam and this man to shelter with the rest of your party. Pete and I will hold them off.'

'Pete?' David echoed blankly.

On cue, a big, muscled man in a bloodied white T-shirt emerged from the humid darkness; Adam recognized him from his fleeting moments of consciousness on the *Hula Queen*. Pete was wielding a high-tech crossbow with a telescopic sight, but he was shaking all over.

'Move,' Chen urged David.

'I can't,' Lisa whispered, eyes wet and wide with terror. 'My legs, the *pain*...' She took a few faltering steps but then fell to the ground next to Harm's unmoving body – just as Loner came staggering back from his battle in the tropical brush behind them. One of his sickle-claws was broken and his left arm hung limply at his side.

Chen whirled round at the sudden movement. 'Pete, get that one, it's wounded.'

'No!' Adam shouted. As Pete pulled on the crossbow's trigger Adam knocked his arm. The bolt went wide and clattered into the bone pit. *Those Brutes couldn't kill him*, Adam thought fiercely, *and you're not going to finish the job.*

'What the . . . ?' Pete rounded on Adam.

'Agent Chen, that's Loner!' The words spilled from Adam's mouth in a frantic rush. 'The raptor in the video who helped Lisa and the others, don't hurt him—'

'*Soft-skins!*'

The unearthly shriek heralded the coming of more Brutes in pursuit of Chen's group, crashing from out of the foliage. Pete shot a bolt into the quill-covered chest of the one closest. It yanked out the arrow shaft as though it were a splinter and bared its hideous teeth – just as Chen let rip again with the shotgun. The monster's open mouth seemed to explode in a hail of shattered teeth, but even as it screamed its pain, the Brute behind it dived forwards. It was smaller than the others with a hunched, misshapen back.

But it was no less vicious.

It jarred the crossbow from Pete's sweaty grip with a spray of acid and then the sickle-claw on its hind leg swung up and cut him almost in half with a single slash. As Pete's lifeless body thudded to the ground, Chen screamed and fired two more shots at the hunchback, driving it back.

Adam was almost sick. He turned, trying to hide his eyes from the horror – and saw Loner stagger-ing closer to the group. The Vel's face was a mass of weeping blisters. He pushed past Adam and stood in front of him protectively, squaring up to the Brutes.

'Wait!' Loner rasped.

The two Brutes hesitated.

'They'll kill him,' whispered Lisa, as Harm's dark eyes opened – and quickly clouded. She put a hand over her lips, stifled a gasp as the Brute with the bloodied mouth took a step closer to Loner.

'It is *him*,' the creature spat.

'This is the wrong way. The wrong way.' Loner tried to stand tall, and the gashes in his blood-caked chest reopened. 'I know you want these . . . *people* as bait. Bait to lure out Vels so you can attack. Kill. But my plan is better. Listen to me.'

'Where are our brother and sister?' Broken-Teeth demanded. 'They circled round to cut off the soft-skins' escape.'

'I had . . . to stop them,' hissed Loner. 'But I spared their lives. They will heal.'

The Brute's jaws swung open. '*You* will not . . .'

Loner shook his head. 'Hurt us and I will not help you destroy the Vels.'

'You *are* a Vel,' snarled Broken-Teeth. 'Not of our pack.'

'Not of any pack,' said Loner hoarsely. 'The two I stopped . . . they were not clever like you. I knew they would not listen. Only a born leader is smart enough to listen . . .'

Broken-Teeth said nothing, glaring at Loner.

'Only a leader would understand my plan.'

He's buying it, Adam realized, holding his breath. *Loner's buttering him up and he's buying it.*

'Wait.' The squat, hunchbacked Brute who'd killed Pete pushed in front of its gap-toothed brother. 'You,' it whispered, cruel eyes fixed on Harmony. 'You.'

Adam swallowed hard. Was the Brute going to attack?

'Perfect,' it hissed. 'Sweet. Yes. You are mine.'

Harm's breath came out in a whimper. 'No.'

'You are *mine*.' Hunchback nodded its head. 'Sweet. Perfect. You . . .'

'Stop it!' Harm shouted, as Lisa gripped hold of her hand and the Brute went on muttering. 'Stop it!'

Broken-Teeth shoved the hunchbacked raptor back into the bushes, one clawed hand raised in warning. Then it turned back to Loner, expectantly.

'These soft-skins you were chasing have no scent,' Loner went on, jerking his head towards Chen and Stone. 'I know why.'

Stone glanced at Chen. '*How* does it know?' he breathed.

'Spare us and I will share that secret with your group,' Loner went on. 'Then the Vels will not scent you. You can kill with no warning.'

'Warning,' echoed Chen, quietly looking round at each of his group, opening his hand behind his back. Adam saw with a jolt that the man held a grenade in his palm. A metal pin fell silently to the grass at his feet.

Adam felt panic rising, saw it mirrored in Harm's eyes; she'd seen the pin too. What was Chen doing?

As Loner took another cautious step towards Broken-Teeth, lowering his head, the hunchback grew agitated. 'Kneel,' it rasped, pointing its claws at Loner. 'Kneel low.'

Loner reacted as though struck in his black-burned face.

'Kneel low! The loner—'

'Quiet,' Broken-Teeth snarled at its brother.

'*Back!*' bellowed Chen. The world seemed to slow as he lobbed his grenade at Broken-Teeth's legs.

Then the grenade went off low in a blast of roiling flame and a boom so deep it punched Adam's guts and flung his hearing into a ringing void. The shockwave threw him to the ground. The raptors were engulfed in smoke and flame, lost from sight.

Loner included.

Lost in shock, Adam felt someone grab his arm. Lisa. Even with her burned legs she had the strength and sense to guide him. She looked as shocked and scared as he felt.

The whole ragged bunch of them scrambled into the cover of the forest, breaking through the thick foliage, leaving the bone pit far behind. But Adam knew he could never outrun the image of the grenade going off so close to Loner, engulfing him in the fireball.

Slowly, Adam's hearing returned, sound rattling loosely as though distorting through speakers. He could hear Harm, sprawled on the ground, weeping: 'You killed Loner! He looked out for us, he helped us.'

'We'd all be dead without him,' David stormed.

'You'd all be dead back there if I hadn't done

something,' Chen shot back. 'You saw what those things did to Pete.'

'Maybe – maybe Loner's all right,' Lisa said.

'He was beat up pretty bad before.' Adam leaned hard against a tree, pushing back wet hair from his forehead. 'But then, Geneflow breed their wildlife tough as tanks. He could've made it.'

'Oh yeah,' Chen said impatiently. 'I was forgetting you're the dinosaur whisperer.'

Adam glared at him. 'That's why you kidnapped me, wasn't it? 'Cause of what I know?'

'Well *I* know we all need to rest up and *shut* up for a bit,' said Stone, examining Lisa's blistered legs. He pulled a little bottle from the battered medicine bag on the ground. 'I have some iodine here. I'm afraid it'll sting real bad . . .'

Lisa threw back her head and gasped through gritted teeth as the antiseptic made good on his promise.

'Harm needs some too,' said Adam, clocking the blood on her neck.

She shook her head and winced. 'I'm fine,' she insisted.

'You're not,' said Stone. 'Those monsters will smell the bleeding a mile away.' He passed Harm the bottle. 'Better get the spray, John. If any of those creatures survived the blast, we all need to be invisible.'

'Invisible. If only . . .' said Lisa.

Harm nodded as she dabbed the iodine on her wound. 'And now . . . with no Loner watching out for us . . .'

'Look. And listen.' Chen pulled a canister from out of a Ziploc bag. 'But don't bother sniffing. This is the anti-stink spray Geneflow use to keep their staff off the dino-radar. Deadens your scent to the wildlife's smell receptors or something.'

Lisa stared. 'You mean we really *can* hide from the raptors?'

'Those Brutes back there seemed to have your scent in their nostrils well enough,' David observed.

Stone shook his head. 'They didn't smell us, they *saw* us,' he explained. 'They'd gotten hold of Brad. We tried to tail them to see if he was alive . . .'

'But he wasn't, was he?' Adam shut his eyes as he remembered Brad's agonized screams back on the beach.

'I had to know for sure,' Chen muttered, as though trying to convince himself he'd been right. 'Pete was against going, but now . . .'

'That canister,' Adam said, changing the subject. 'How'd you get hold of it?'

'Three cans were recovered from the Geneflow base at Fort Ponil you know so well,' Chen told him. 'Forensics even salvaged some intel on its development.' He shrugged. 'I tried it out with some of the guys, hunting deer in the Rockies. The stuff works . . .' He sprayed Adam, who coughed as the aerosol engulfed him. 'I don't know how much is enough or how much we've got left. Had another canister but it got lost in the water.' He shook his head bitterly. 'I felt so sure this stuff would give us the drop on the wildlife.'

'You never change, John,' Stone said, not unkindly. 'When did your hunches *ever* work out? You always did spend a second thinking and a week feeling sorry.'

Adam watched as Chen sprayed Harmony from top to toe. 'What brought you here?' he demanded.

'The tide and a strong front crawl,' Chen replied. 'Lucky for the doc he clung onto a life vest in the water as well as his bag of tricks, helped him wash up on shore.'

Stone snorted. 'I've been washed up for years.'

'This isn't a joke. You know exactly what I mean.' Adam could hear his voice getting high and squeaky, fought to bring it down lower. 'You've kidnapped me and my dad, you've got your own friends killed, and I just need to know—'

'Why I came here.' Chen moved on to spray Lisa, who screwed up her eyes and tried not to choke. 'Well, it's simple. I need to talk to Josephs.'

'Why?' Adam demanded.

Chen shook his head. 'Remember I told you that there was someone in the FBI I *knew* had taken bribes from Josephs?' He looked weary, so weary. 'Well, that someone . . . was me.'

Adam's stomach turned cartwheels. He stared at Chen in a kind of uncomprehending disappointment. 'You . . . you're working for her?'

David leaned forward angrily and gripped Chen's wrist. 'What is this?'

Chen shook him off and looked at Adam, and his eyes seemed wet. 'Look, I made a mistake a while back, all right? That's what this is all about.' He pushed the spray can into David's hands and sat on the grass, hugging his knees. 'Almost three years ago I was investigating an industrial espionage case. High-tech secrets going missing. Josephs' name was in the frame, and my team were *that* close to nailing her. She found out . . .' He shrugged. 'And so she bought me off.'

'You took her money? Let her get away with it?' Adam realized that he and Harm, David and Lisa were fixing Chen with the same look of disgust.

'It was so much cash . . .' Chen was gently rocking, resting his head on his knees. 'And I thought Josephs was stealing the info just to sell it, you know?'

'Oh, that's all right then,' said David sarcastically.

'Because every one of you chose the right thing to do your whole lives long, didn't you?' Chen shook his head, quieter now. 'You know what I'm saying – it's all fat cat companies and their bottom lines, right? No one gets hurt, no one dies. That's what I thought, anyways.' He looked down at his feet. 'Then I saw what had gone down at Fort Ponil. The carnage there. The corpses. That crazy stuff we dug up about . . . about *dinosaurs*. And when I found Josephs' name attached . . .' He looked up at Adam and finally it was as if there were someone alive and feeling behind those dark eyes. 'I needed to know exactly what it was I had helped her make possible, you know? Find out how big this is. How responsible I was.'

'And to see if you could cover up your involvement,' Adam realized, his loathing for Chen growing by the moment. 'That's why you didn't go to your bosses. Why you dragged my dad out here in secret as your science adviser, why you brought no proper back-up.'

Harm was giving Chen looks hard enough to bludgeon. 'You helped this whole nightmare to happen!'

'I did nothing to stop it,' Chen conceded calmly. 'And I know now that I should've done. I didn't want anyone to die . . . Believe me, if I could do things over and do them differently . . .'

'I guess . . . I do believe you,' said Lisa.

David shook his head. 'Always seeing the good in people, huh?'

'I bet he came here for the same reason the people we loved came here from Death Row,' she argued. 'For a shot at redemption. To start over.'

I'm sure you'd like to believe that, thought Adam privately. *But if those prisoners were on Death Row to start with, they could've come here just because they had nothing to lose.*

'Death Row?' Chen looked at Lisa. 'Like your husband?'

'He wasn't killed in jail like you thought,' Adam cut in. 'Him and a whole lot of others like him got taken here by Geneflow—'

'And they were fed to the raptors,' said Harm. 'End of.'

Stone looked at David, his face haunted. 'Why, for pity's sake?'

No one had an answer.

Chen rubbed his temples. 'Well, you can all hate me as much as you want. But at least I'm bringing the cavalry.'

Adam frowned. 'What do you mean?'

'I mean, the *Pahalu* will be sailing back to Hawaii by tomorrow morning.'

'What?' Adam felt shaken. 'But Dad wouldn't leave me.'

'And my guys out there wouldn't leave me and Doc Stone behind if they had a choice. But what can they do with those things in the water guarding the way?' Chen shook his head. 'They're under strict instructions that if there's no word from me within thirty-six hours they're to turn tail and get in touch with our old friend Marrs at the United Nations.' He shrugged. 'I lost my radio in the big wash-out, so there you go. Cavalry.'

'How long will that cavalry take to get here?' Harm asked slowly.

'Days? Weeks even.' David sprayed himself with the anti-stink. 'And the experiment might finish any time. When it does, Josephs and Geneflow will bail. Whoever comes here will find nothing.'

'Except us.' Lisa's voice sounded so fragile the breeze could've bruised it.

Except for our chewed-up bones, thought Adam. He wanted to cry at the thought of his dad sailing further and further away without him.

'Wait,' said Stone. 'I think something's coming.'

Chen grabbed his shotgun and pressed a pistol into Stone's hand. Stone passed it to David, who accepted it grimly.

Adam looked at Harm. She was holding her breath, and he realized he was doing the same. David was holding the gun so tight his knuckles looked set to pop through the skin. A stealthy, rustling noise crept into his ringing ears.

Stone was right. Something was drawing nearer.

14: Sleepless Night

Not again, Adam thought, coldness and exhaustion filling his bones. *Can't go through it again.*

'So much for your spray,' David sneered at Chen.

'We've been making enough noise to wake the dead,' Stone whispered tersely, 'let alone a pack of lizards born to hunt.'

Chen aimed his shotgun.

The rustling of vegetation stopped, and laboured breathing sounded in its place. 'Do not shoot,' came a soft, mournful voice from the darkness.

'Loner?' Lisa breathed.

Harm turned to Adam, incredulous. 'He's alive.'

'If *he's* alive . . .' Chen gripped his shotgun all the tighter and edged closer to Stone. 'What about the others?'

'I am alone.'

Adam got up as Loner stalked closer, but his smile of relief soon faded. The raptor was barely recognizable. His hide was burned black. Along one side, his stubby shield of shoulder quills was a mass of shattered stumps. One arm hung uselessly by his side, caked in mud. His breathing came in hard, stubborn wheezes and his eyes smouldered dull yellow.

'Thank God you're all right,' Lisa said, struggling to get up. 'After all you've done for us . . .' It looked for a moment like she was going to hug him, but instead she hovered awkwardly. 'You are all right, aren't you?'

Loner bobbed his head. 'Others bore the worst of the blast. I will heal. In time, so will they. We are very hard to kill.' He looked balefully at Chen. 'Very hard.'

'If the Z. raptors are anything like the Z. rex, their cells repair really quickly,' Adam said. 'I think that's how they're made – regenerating the original fossils, or something.'

'Little beyond my twelfth-grade science,' David said. 'Loner, we— We're so sorry this happened.'

Adam nodded and turned to Chen. 'Aren't we?'

Chen didn't look at Loner, but he nodded. 'Sure. I didn't come here to kill off the good guys.'

Loner did not comment on the half-hearted apology. 'We must leave this place,' he said. 'Vels are coming. The explosion . . .'

'Of course,' said David. 'This part of the jungle will be swarming with raptors.'

'They can't smell us now,' Adam reminded him.

'They won't need to.' Harm shuddered. 'They'll most likely trip over us.'

'Where do we go?' asked Lisa.

'We just keep moving,' said Chen. 'Find some higher ground with cover, so we can see these raptor things coming, but they can't see us.'

'I know a place,' said Loner, straightening his shoulders with some difficulty. 'Sheltered. Overlooking the Vel camp.'

Lisa blanched. 'We want to get that close?'

'It's not just the Vel camp,' David reminded her, looking at Chen. 'Geneflow built their headquarters beneath it.'

'Yeah?' Chen nodded. 'I'd like to check that out.'

'I suppose it's safer to keep moving.' Stone got up. 'At least if these Vel things are out searching the jungle, there'll be fewer minding their store.'

'They've got guards, a barricade and all kinds of stuff,' Adam informed him. 'I saw through these.' He pulled out Chen's binoculars. 'The Brutes must've found them washed up on the beach, and Loner found them near their camp at the north cliffs.'

'They were spying on the Vels too, huh?' Chen took the binoculars with a smile and looked round at the others. 'Well, I think maybe we should take a closer look. Who's coming?'

Harm answered with a shrug, David and Lisa with weary nods. Adam looked at Stone, who gave a weak smile of encouragement.

Loner was first to move, turning and limping into the jungle. 'This way,' he said.

The hike seemed to last for ever. By its end, Adam was hot, tired and so exhausted he wanted to go to sleep and never wake up again.

Which could happen so easily, he thought, as night settled over the huddle of survivors and their new camp in the high ground.

The group had formed a nervous, huddled crocodile through the palms and bushes and trailed for hours, like kindergarten kids on the mother of all field trips. David tried to help Lisa walk but was clearly all but exhausted himself. Adam saw the unhappy look on his face as he watched Chen eventually carry Lisa like she weighed next to nothing. *Guess he's been the alpha male for months*, thought Adam, *and now . . .*

All too often Loner would direct them to stand still, waiting for Vel patrols to pass or lone Brutes to crash on their way.

The only wildlife they'd actually stumbled upon had been a single ostrich in a clearing. Loner drooled, but was in no condition to chase it down. Then Chen had surprised everyone by stopping the procession, reaching into his pack and pulling out a chunky yellow pistol.

'Stun gun,' he'd whispered, taken careful aim and fired.

Electrodes had flown from the barrel and hooked into the ostrich's skin; stunned by a sudden pulse of electrical current, the bird had dropped. Before it could regain its senses, Loner had shambled over and crammed it into his powerful jaws. As his teeth tore greedily through tissue and bone, he'd given Chen a look that might have held surprise, and so had Adam.

Chen's only comment: 'Target practice.'

It looked to Adam now as though someone had been using the night for the same purpose, its blackness peppered with stars like a billion tiny bright bullet holes. Too wired to sleep, Adam stared up at the stars from a makeshift hammock of fleshy leaves and jungle vines strung high between two sturdy palms, wishing he were far away from here.

So much for day one on Raptor Island, he thought.

Loner had led them to a vantage point overlooking the Vel camp. Not only did the camp have thick concrete walls for protection, it was surrounded on three sides by cliffs and the sea – most likely the reason the US military had chosen the site during World War Two in the first place, in case of Japanese attack. David reckoned it was probably no more than a kilometre around the coast from the Brutes' home turf, while Harm suspected the distance was closer to a million when you had to divert through the jungle as they had just done.

As for Adam, he'd felt happier when the Vel camp had been a hazy image through binoculars. Looking down from here, the striped raptors seemed close enough to touch.

Loner had gone away, sniffing for scent trails, making doubly sure that this place and its approaches were not in regular use. Reunited with his binoculars, Chen had spent an age scrutinizing the area while the other survivors had got busy securing their makeshift camp as best they could, rigging up early warning systems using bundles of sticks and jungle-vine tripwires. But creepily, the Vels' own security was more high-tech. To Adam's astonishment, floodlights kicked on as dusk settled, illuminating the camp in a harsh yellow glare. The scaly monsters cast thick, misshapen shadows behind their barricades of scrap metal, some of them even wearing plates of metal as improvised armour.

'It's like they're expecting an attack,' David had observed. 'Maybe they know the Brutes have been spying on them.'

'There were no floodlights when we scouted this

way before,' Lisa agreed. 'Something's got them rattled.'

If only Zed were here, Adam thought. *He'd save me.* He wished for the huge reptile to come swooping down from out of the sky on his impossible wings, bearing Dad on his back, and ached with loneliness.

And then Adam thought about Loner. Like Zed, Loner was a beast at odds with the world around him; humans and dinosaurs were never meant to co-exist. And yet . . . Weirdly, it felt to Adam as if there was already some kind of bond between him and Loner. The raptor had carried him and fought for him and almost died for him without thought or hesitation. Was it only because the Think-Send technology used to train him had touched him somehow with Adam's humanity?

Or by some fluke of nature or science, had this beast evolved beyond the others to develop a con-science?

Adam shuddered. So many dinosaurs, clustered in one place. This island was a living nightmare, and he felt a thousand miles from the sleep he so badly craved. *I need to evolve the ability to switch off my brain.*

As the youngest members of the party, he and Harm had been allowed to sleep first before taking their turn on watch. But the slightest noise seemed to travel like a bullet in the night air. Even now, Adam could hear Dr Stone's voice carry from the clearing, low and fragile: 'Those things are just reptiles . . . How can they be doing this?'

'If Geneflow built a whole underground base beneath that thing they must have used tons of construction gear,' said David. 'I suppose the raptors found some of it and worked out how to use—'

'I mean, how can they be so advanced?' Stone interrupted. 'So prepared?'

Lisa shrugged. 'Geneflow made them that way, honey.'

'It's what they'll be made to do once this little experiment is over that scares me.' Chen sounded grave. 'If only we could get inside that base and—'

'No chance,' David muttered. 'Even if they can't smell us, they'd see us coming a mile off.'

'And if they see Loner they'll kill him just for coming back,' said Lisa. 'Where is he? He's been ages . . .'

'Adam?' Harm's voice came out of the silvery darkness. 'You awake?'

'Wide awake.' He looked across and dimly saw a figure lying in a hammock fashioned from an old blanket between two neighbouring palms. 'I don't know how you've slept at all on this island.'

'Yeah, well, total exhaustion's quite good for that.' She gave a low whistle. 'You know what? It's Christmas Eve.'

Adam frowned. 'It is?'

'Maybe we should go down and crash the grown-ups' party.' Harm sighed. 'Sure is comforting, having all these grown-ups around to look after us, huh?'

Adam imagined his unwrapped present to his dad lying back at his New York hotel room. A pair of gloves, to ward off the Manhattan cold. Tears suddenly prickled at the back of his eyes and he dashed them away, glad of the darkness. Would the staff at the hotel realize the room had been empty for days? Would they have told the police? Maybe Jeremy Marrs had tried to get hold of Mr Adlar or even Chen and realized they were missing . . .

Soon the Pahalu *will be headed back to Hawaii. Dad will tell Dr Marrs where the island is. They can get help . . .*

The notion seemed as ridiculous as a happy Christmas.

'It's really selfish,' Adam muttered, 'but I wish my dad was here.'

Harm stretched in her hammock. 'Guess he's always been around for you, right?'

'Well . . . most of the time. His work's always been really important to him, and sometimes it sort of takes over . . .' Adam felt a pang of guilt. 'But he's great. He's there for me and I'm there for him.'

'What about your mom?'

Adam stared on up at the stars. 'She died way back.'

Harm said nothing, one hand idly playing with her ragged braids. 'It's good you have your dad around. Mine went to jail when I was just five.'

'What did he do?' asked Adam.

'Killed two cops. He was robbing some place, they surprised him . . .' Harm was silent for a time. 'You know, I grew up hating him so much. And it was weird – the more I hated him, the more I missed him, and that fed into the way I hated him, and . . .' The words dried up into slow, steady breathing. Adam was wondering how best to fill the silence when Harm spoke again, quieter, huskier. 'My mom never let me see him. Wanted a clean start.'

'You never visited him?'

'No one to take me. I wrote him, sometimes. He always wrote back. I sent him pictures, sort of me goofing around or dressing up. He said he hoped I'd be able to visit some day by myself when I was old enough and he would get to see me all grown up.' Harm snorted. 'I kidded myself he really cared.'

'Of course he cared,' said Adam. 'You're his daughter.'

'You know . . .' Harm took a deep breath as if steeling herself. 'He always called me his . . . his . . .'

Adam waited. 'His what?'

'Never mind.' Her voice sounded thicker, as though tears were close. 'That Brute . . . the way he looked at me. Spoke to me.'

'Sweet and perfect . . .' Adam shivered. 'Like you were his ideal meal or something.'

'Don't.'

'That whole pack of Brutes had stuff wrong with them, did you see?' Adam saw Harm's head nod in the moonlight. 'Hunchbacks or one eye or half-lame or just crazy or whatever.'

'So they formed a club. I'm happy for them.'

'But why would their queen send the weakest in the pack to get us?' Adam persisted. 'If we're, like, a big part of her plan for getting the Vels—'

'Even the weakest of those things are a thousand times tougher than we are.' Harm shifted in her hammock. 'Do you buy Agent Chen's story of why he brought you here?' she asked suddenly. 'That he'd risk so many lives and his own too, and splash out on two boats just to find out how much of a bad boy he's been? I mean, I can give you the names of twenty care workers who'll tell you I got trust issues, but, man . . .'

Adam felt uneasy. 'Chen's seen what was left of another Geneflow base after a Z. rex tore it apart. No one could let stuff like that happen again if they felt responsible, could they?'

'He and his buddy out there drugged you, Adam. Is that what the good guys do?' The edge to Harm's voice was hard as the starlight. 'What if Agent Chen knows Josephs a little better than he makes out?

Maybe he thinks no one can stop what Geneflow's doing and wants to save his own ass by getting in with them?'

'No, he couldn't want that . . . could he?' Adam sighed. 'I don't know. I don't know anything.'

Suddenly, the crash of brushwood trampled underfoot ghosted through the night. *Oh, God, they've found us.* Adam turned awkwardly in the thick palm leaves, as the small jungle clearing underneath them rustled with strained whispers and hissing voices. But then Chen's muted call sounded over them. 'Looks like our tame dinosaur just got home.'

Adam saw movement in the darkness; a mound of dark scales patterned with scars, hunched over.

'Loner?' Lisa sounded like a worried mother. 'Did something happen? Your face . . .'

'It is only mud,' came the quiet hiss. 'It soothes my wounds.'

'You were hurt again?' Lisa persisted.

'Vel patrol saw me. I led it away. Into Brute territory.' He paused, his breath low and laboured. 'The Brute who was shot in the teeth found me.'

Chen spoke up, sharp and suspicious: 'You led it here?'

He shook his head. 'The Brutes . . . are making ready for total war on the Vels.'

'Then they'll be swarming over this whole area,'

said Stone. 'We've come to the most dangerous part of the island.'

A hubbub of low, fearful voices started up.

'We'd better get down there,' Adam said to Harm.

She nodded. 'We should hear things properly.'

Adam climbed down the tree, an awkward, graceless thing, half-numb with dread at what he was to hear.

He couldn't help feeling that his first night on the island might very well be his last.

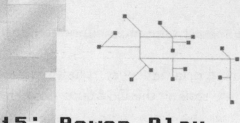

15: Power Play

Harm led the way into the clearing. Adam could
see her dark skin was glistening with sweat in the
moonlight. He tried to look cool but it was hard
with his heart hammering in his chest.

'I'm sorry we woke you guys,' said Lisa quietly.

'We couldn't sleep anyway.' Adam took a long
look at Loner. The raptor's arm still hung limply at
his side, and the mud was covering the gorier parts
of his face, chest and side, but he was looking a lot
better than he had been earlier.

Loner crossed to Chen's pack and plucked out
the can of anti-stink with his good hand.

'Hey!' Chen protested.

'The Brutes need this,' Loner said simply. 'Then
they can help us while they help themselves.'

Chen looked into the injured raptor's eyes but
couldn't keep the contact. 'What're you talking
about?'

Loner looked round at the nervous, huddled
humans. 'It is Vels who have hunted your fellow

survivors. Vels who have kept them alive, waiting. Waiting for the feast.' He paused, his breathing softer now, each word cold and clear. 'The Brutes let them do so. Now the time of the feast is coming, the Brute queen will *take* those prisoners by force.'

Harm stared at him. 'What?'

'Who says they're stupid.' David let out a low whistle. 'They let the Vels do the hard work and then steam in and clear out the survivors in one hit. Two raptor tribes going head to head, and we're the prize. Maybe that's what the experiment is all about. Like a test.'

'Sure . . . what is it they say?' Lisa remembered: 'Survival of the fittest.'

'But the Vels aren't just going to hand over their prisoners to the Brutes, right?' said Adam. 'There'll be full-on war.'

'Death or glory, huh?' said Stone. 'Maybe these things are more like people than we think.'

Loner held up the spray can. 'They wanted to use you as bait to help them get the Vels – until I told them about this.'

'That stuff could make the battle go a whole lot better for the Brutes,' David realized. 'They could attack the Vels without any warning.'

'But there's nowhere near enough spray for the whole pack,' Harm pointed out.

'So, just spray their biggest and baddest,' said

David. 'Send them creeping up for a surprise attack.'

'It'll be carnage,' Stone muttered. 'Total carnage – and here's us with no more spray and nowhere to hide.'

'There might be somewhere,' said Adam, hope sputtering inside him. 'What if we could get inside the Vel base while the raptors are busy fighting? Free the other people they've taken . . .'

Harm raised her eyebrows. 'I thought it was me who got hit on the head today?'

But David was looking at him thoughtfully. 'That would mess up their experiment, all right.'

Adam nodded enthusiastically. 'I just thought – the Vel camp is right on top of Geneflow's base, and Loner knows the codes to get inside.'

Chen reacted. 'He does?'

'Sure he does.' Adam turned to Loner. 'You got in a few times before your pack turned against you. Right?'

The wounded raptor gave a cautious nod.

'Even if we could get past those creatures and reach Geneflow's base, it'll be defended,' Stone argued. 'She must have guards—'

'And we've got guns,' said Chen. 'They might not work on raptors but they'll sure work on people. No one knows that better than you, Doc.'

'And if you could set free the other survivors, there'd be lots of us,' Lisa added.

'Lots wanting payback,' Harm agreed.

'On this island, it's always been them and us.' David took a deep breath. 'I'd sooner there were more of "us".'

'I don't know that we want too many people trying to get inside,' Chen argued. 'Whatever happens in there, it's not gonna be a walk in the park. This is gonna be a two-man op, maybe three, tops.'

'Three men and a dinosaur?' Stone shook his head. 'John, you're just rushing in again without thinking.'

'You said yourself we got nowhere to hide out here,' Chen said hotly, ignoring the others shushing him. 'If we get inside, if we can get to Josephs . . .'

'If, if, if,' Stone muttered.

'Doc . . .' Chen crossed over to the pale, greying doctor and put his hands on the man's shoulders. '*When* we do that . . . everything we've been through will have counted for something. Right?'

Stone looked away and said nothing.

'Just say it worked,' Lisa breathed. 'If the raptors wiped each other out and we could stop Geneflow . . .' She took Harm's hand and squeezed. 'Oh, honey, can you imagine?'

Adam looked at Loner, who was standing in the middle of the excited group, battered and alone, looking down at the canister. He felt a stir of dismay in the rush of feelings going through him. The outcast beast had done so much for them, and here they were expecting way more of him. 'What do *you* think, Loner?' he asked. 'You're the only one who's seen inside that base . . .'

David nodded. 'Do you think you can get everyone in?'

'Some, perhaps,' Loner said. 'Dangerous.'

'But this dino-ruck is gonna be keeping Geneflow's guys busy,' Chen argued. 'Especially with scent-free Brutes rolling around, right? Josephs'll be trying to keep on top of things, she'll be distracted. It's our best shot.'

'Let's face it,' said Harm. 'It's our only shot.'

'But . . . I just thought.' Adam placed a hand carefully on the raptor's injured arm. 'If you go back to the Brutes and give them the spray, they'll have what they want. Can you trust them to let you go again after what you did?'

'I know about the Vel defences,' Loner said. 'I can switch off their lights, make safe their traps . . . if I live.'

'Now you have no scent,' said David quietly, 'do you think you stand a chance?'

'If we are to get inside Geneflow, I must,' said Loner. 'But . . .'

'The dinosaur has a but,' Stone muttered.

'I will need help.' He suddenly swung his head round to face Adam, the moonlight casting the mud-packed, scarred side of his face into sharp shadow. 'The floodlights are run by a generator, protected by the tower . . .'

Adam looked at Chen. 'The same tower we saw from the sea?'

'Like a metal chimney at the edge of the trees.' Chen tapped his binoculars. 'I saw it. Didn't look to be guarded.'

'Why bother to build a tower for it outside when they could put it indoors under concrete?' Harm wondered.

'If it runs on gasoline it'll be giving off carbon monoxide fumes,' David told her. 'Deadly gas indoors, not good.'

'The generator is protected by thick metal, bolted and welded together all round,' Loner continued. 'Only the Council can get inside with special keys. But there are small gaps.' He lowered his head as if aware what he was asking. 'Gaps that maybe a child can get through.'

Adam felt his world tilt. As the youngest here he'd been getting used to the idea of being the last to be consulted on anything. Now suddenly he was supposed to play a vital part?

'You can't send kids into that place!' Stone said fiercely.

'I've got no more grenades,' said Chen, 'no other way to wreck the damn thing.'

'Assuming this generator's nothing too fancy, sand in the air intake ought to be enough to blow the whole thing,' David reasoned. 'Wouldn't take long. Could *I* get inside?'

Loner shook his head sadly.

'Well, I'm not a kid, but I'm about the scrawniest here,' Harm declared, her chin pushed out. 'I knew starving for three months was a good idea. If someone tells me what to do . . .'

Adam felt suddenly exposed. 'I . . . I'll go too,' he heard himself saying. 'I'm not much bigger than you. Two of us can cover each other, work faster.'

'And double the risk,' Stone said. 'John, you can't use kids to fight a battle like this!'

'Well, we're not exactly drowning in choices, are we?' Chen shot back.

'You're not in charge,' David insisted, but with more petulance than authority. 'We . . . we could run to the other end of the island while the raptors bite chunks out of each other, *keep* running from any who survive—'

'And what happens to the other people being held there?' Harm demanded. 'We leave them to die?' She shook her head. 'I don't care who's in charge. I'm through running. If Loner can set it up . . . I want to do this.'

I want to be as brave as you, Adam thought. 'I'm in too.'

With a shaky sigh, David nodded his head a fraction. Lisa closed her eyes and Adam saw tears streaking her face. No one else said anything.

Loner turned with the can of spray and loped away into the darkness to broker the deal.

To begin the endgame.

Adam surprised himself by falling asleep despite his nerves. He jolted awake in his hammock when a hand squeezed his ankle. But it was only Harm.

'Loner's back,' she whispered. 'It's close to three and we've got to move.'

'Did he . . . ?'

She nodded, and looked away. 'Deal's done. We've got to go. Right now.'

Adam found the sleep had done little to refresh him. His body ached with the physical strain of the last twenty-four hours, but fear kept him alert. He followed with the group behind Loner, who moved with impressive grace through the foliage despite his injuries, barely making a sound. Chen was next in line, wielding his shotgun. Adam, Harm, David and Dr Stone took it in turns to help Lisa make the journey.

Lisa looked at Stone as he helped her over a fallen tree. 'Why'd you ever come here, honey?' she whispered.

Stone wiped sweat through his wispy hair but didn't reply.

'You said you owed Chen after he helped you out with some trouble at the Bureau,' Adam prompted him.

Stone shrugged. 'I used to have a drink problem. Made some . . . some errors of judgement in my work. I should've been fired. Chen covered up for me, helped me get a discharge on medical grounds.'

'You'd helped out some buddies of mine in the past, Doc,' Chen said quietly. 'So I helped you.'

'What is this,' said Harm, 'last confessions?'

'It's all about loyalty with me, girl,' Chen said. 'Us and them. I'll do my best to watch out for all of you, but that means you do what I say, OK?'

'Like Pete did,' David muttered.

Loner stopped abruptly, bringing an end to the conversation. 'We are close to the camp.'

Lisa hugged herself. 'If the Vels smell us now . . .'

Loner's tail swished from side to side — then he pushed it into the ground in front of them. The grass and brushwood gave way and crashed to the ground some distance below.

'They have some old-fashioned tricks as well as electronic ones,' Stone said shakily.

'One trap down,' Chen muttered. 'The Brutes are gonna love you.'

'The Brutes will be close,' said Loner, a level of

urgency in the hushed, hissing tones. 'Can you hear the generator?'

Adam concentrated, and even his heart seemed to bump more quietly as he caught a faint, trailing whine of power. His eyes met Harm's. She nodded a fraction.

'The safest way to the tower is through the trees,' Loner went on. 'They will help keep you in shadow until you can get inside the tower.'

Adam looked at David. 'If we *can* get in, what exactly do we need to do to cut the power?'

'The running engine makes heat,' David whispered. 'Air is blown through the motor housing . . . by a fan connected to the driveshaft.'

'Whoa,' Harm said. 'What are we, mechanics?'

'The air inlet should be marked,' said David. 'Prise it open and pour in sand like I said. It'll be sucked right inside the motor and mess it up good.'

Chen looked at Adam and Harm. 'You guys OK with that?'

'I guess,' said Harm, and Adam nodded.

'Now, listen,' Chen went on. 'When the power cuts out, every raptor around's gonna make straight for that tower – so you gotta split fast. Your nearest cover will be to the east – a square outbuilding with a fence around it, close to the cliff-edge.'

'Loner will lead the rest of us there in the darkness,' David added, his smile too small to be of much reassurance. 'Then we'll all be ready to move as soon as things kick off.'

Lisa looked at Harm and Adam, full of concern. 'Should we maybe walk you there?'

'I will guide them,' Loner declared.

'Good luck,' Stone whispered.

His heart doing its best to slither up his throat, Adam followed Harm and Loner through the jungle, an eerie landscape of spindly trunks and creepers. At one point, they had to freeze as a Vel on sentry duty moved nimbly past. Its crimson skin looked blood-black in the moonlight and its yellow eyes were like lanterns. It peered about, then moved on.

Harm released a long breath. 'We were crazy to agree to this.'

Adam nodded. He felt like his life had become one of the 'Choose Your Own Adventure' books he'd loved reading as a kid. A choice on every page, leading you forward and back through the pages. One route might lead you to an ending where you triumphed in your adventure and everything turned out for the best.

Another might leave you dead in tatters halfway.

Loner led the way to a thick, sprawling tree and then turned to face Adam. 'I can go no further.' His whisper caught thickly at the back of his throat. 'Not enough cover.' The raptor carefully pressed a

clawed hand against his shoulder, and Adam felt a
jolt at how quickly he'd come to trust this sinister-
looking stranger. Loner touched Harm's shoulder
too, let it linger there a little longer. Then without
further comment, the scaly creature retreated back
into the jungle shadows.

'Least he didn't lick us,' said Harm.

Adam ignored her, taking some crumbs of com-
fort from the gesture of friendship and good luck.
'Let's get this over with.'

The hum of the generator grew louder as Adam
and Harm crept through the jungle. A hard, white
light bathed the clearing up ahead. And there,
maybe twenty metres ahead, a tall, narrow building
was blotting out a swarm of stars in the indigo skies.
It was a patchwork of riveted panels; some made of
steel, which caught a glint of the moon, others
caked in rust.

'Built so tall to keep out other raptors,' Adam
noted. 'Guess even they would have a tough time
climbing sheer metal.'

Harm straightened, a slender silhouette against
the floodlit glade. Aside from the power hum, it was
eerily quiet. 'Should we . . . ?'

'*Go!*' Doubling over, Adam grabbed Harm's hand
and bolted into the brightness. He felt horribly
exposed, convinced at any moment a bloodcurdling
howl would sound and the vicious Vels would fall

upon him and Harm, tearing them to ribbons. The second he reached the thick, protective blackness of the tower's shadow he hurled himself down flat. Harm hit the ground a split-second later.

Panting for breath, his pulse pounding, Adam looked up. The tower was shielding them from sight, but the guarded entrance to the camp and its Vel sentries were maybe a couple of soccer pitches away. How quickly could the raptors cover that distance and discover their intruders?

They both wormed forward on their bellies towards the tower. Adam saw a crude door cut into one side, held in place with bolts and heavy hinges, a lock welded into the metal. 'We're going to have to check right around it for a way in,' he whispered.

'I'll go,' Harm offered.

Adam held his breath, gripping the turf with sweaty palms. The unnatural hum and buzz of the generator filled his ears. He stayed statue-still until she came back – with a frown on her face.

'I saw a way in – we might just make it,' she reported. 'But there's this cable running from the base of the tower . . .'

'So?'

'It stretches towards that outbuilding where Chen told us to wait.' Harm looked at Adam. 'What do you think the Vels need the power for?'

'I don't know. But when we wreck the generator it'll be useless, won't it?'

'But what if it's something important to the Vels and some of them run straight there as well as to the tower?' Harm persisted. 'They'll find the whole lot of us and catch us.' She paused. 'Maybe that's the whole idea. Maybe Chen's setting us up somehow, to save his own skin.'

'They wouldn't let him trash their generator first,' Adam argued. 'Anyway, Loner would kill him before he could escape.'

'Unless the Vels or Geneflow kill Loner first,' Harm retorted. 'We don't know how Josephs watches what goes on here but maybe Chen does. Maybe he's tipped her off that we're coming somehow.'

'So he can get in with Geneflow? Nah—'

'You don't believe me, fine. I hope I'm wrong too.' Harm folded her arms. 'But I say we check it out before we turn out the lights. 'K?'

'All right.' Adam nodded uneasily. 'But we go really carefully.'

Moving slowly and keeping close to the ground, Adam followed Harm as she trailed the cable. The grass was sharp and scratchy. The power lead was old and frayed, patched up with tape, and snaked into the cover of thick jungle for a good fifty metres. Adam hardly breathed. He heard a low, buzzing hum growing louder. Slowly, so slowly, he and Harm edged nearer. Adam had that nightmare sense of being compelled to witness something he'd rather not see, his pounding heart surely outdoing the generator for noise.

Harm tentatively parted some thick, leafy fronds and gave them a narrow view of the mouldering concrete outbuilding, lit only dimly by the reach of the floodlights. Its door stood ajar. A crude fence made from timbers and tree-trunks and lengths of wire edged its perimeter, and this was the source of the humming noise.

An electrified fence, thought Adam. *What are they protecting in there?*

Four quiet beeps sounded, as if buttons were being pressed somewhere close by. The power snapped off. The fence fell quiet, deactivated.

Then a sharp-jawed, reptilian head pushed into sight, a Vel so massive it made Loner seem more like a monitor lizard. It sniffed the air suspiciously outside the door. Its lean body was festooned with quills, each ending in deadly barbs, and it wore the same crude metal armour on its throat, arms and thighs as the sentries at the main entrance.

Then the door to the outbuilding swung open. A ripe smell like manure caught in Adam's throat. In the shadowy light he saw another Vel step out from inside.

'Soon, now,' said the huge, feathered reptile. 'Very soon.'

Adam looked past it, riveted by what was inside the room. He couldn't make sense of it at first: large mounds of dried dung, long grass and palm leaves. Lots of them, maybe twenty. Like enormous nests. And each nest held as many as a half-dozen pale yellow objects the size of footballs, the shape of giant—

'Eggs,' Harm breathed beside him. 'Oh my God, Adam. The raptors have been breeding.'

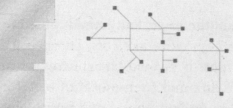

16: Death Strike

Adam lowered his head, fear clawing inside him as the Vel came out through a doorway in the fence and the sentry activated the code again, restarting the electrified fence.

Harm let the bush fronds mask the scene once more and the two of them crawled backwards as quietly as they could, staying low on all fours, following the cable until they were back in the ominous shadow of the humming tower.

Adam looked at her. 'The feast,' he murmured. 'Harm, that's what the Vels who came for us before were talking about. All those human prisoners . . .'

Harm's face was filled with anger. 'It's going to be the bone pit all over again. Those things will hatch and they'll be hungry and . . .'

Adam nodded quickly. She didn't need to go on. 'I don't get it though. Geneflow can clone things, like the ostriches. Why do they need hatchlings when they could just make new raptors?'

''Cause they're sick and they're evil.' Harm

sounded close to hysteria. 'If the raptors can breed they'll spread through cities like rats. Hunt and eat everyone. That's got to be why they want to feed the hatchlings on humans, not ostriches — so they get a taste for human flesh ahead of being released into the real world.'

Adam wasn't convinced. If the raptors took three months each time to reach the point of hatching, how long would it take for a pack to grow big enough to threaten even a major city? People would be wise to the threat and be fighting back—

'Stop just sitting there and come help me,' Harm hissed. She'd got up and was searching carefully for the small gap in the tower's patchwork structure. 'We've got to trash this thing. Let the Brutes get in and smash those eggs for us.'

As Adam got up, an unpleasant penny dropped in his mind. 'Harm, that shelter on the beach at the Brute camp, blocked by boulders. The one you said was new . . .' He swallowed hard. 'D'you think . . . ?'

'That they've got eggs too?' She seemed to deflate a little, resting her head against the rough metal. 'Yeah, figures. That's why they're going to take all the "soft-skins" away with them. To give to *their* hatchlings.'

Adam stood beside her and chanced a squeeze of her hand. 'Whatever Chen's planning, Loner will smell those two Vels at the outbuilding and keep Lisa and David away.'

'And they'll come looking for us.' As if comforted by the thought, she nodded. 'Well, if we're going to do this, first thing we need to do is loosen the big rivet thing.' She pointed above his head. 'Then this metal plate should lift up a bit more, I can slip through and you come in after me.'

Adam nodded and tried to turn the rivet. To his surprise, it wasn't too hard to shift – judging by the heavy scratches in the metal it was a lot harder to tighten things with a handful of claws. Soon he had the rivet out and was able to slide the heavy, rusting metal plate up a couple more centimetres. Harm pulled herself up and wriggled inside. Adam watched her bony legs disappear through the gap. There was the sound of scuffling. 'It's OK. Now, your turn.'

Adam squeezed his head through the narrow gap into the humming, whining darkness and started to struggle inside. He gasped as his ribs caught on the metal, sucked in his stomach as far as it would go. 'Pull me in,' he hissed, and felt Harm's clammy hands fasten on his own. Imagining a raptor coming up behind to bite his legs off, he wriggled all the more furiously until at last he fell in a face-first sprawl on sand and spiky grass; there was no solid floor to the enclosure. He rolled over, disorientated in the thick, rumbling darkness . . .

And his heart slammed to a halt as a red eye shone down at him and hot breath blasted across his face.

Then he realized it was only an operating light to show the generator was running, and the heat was being pumped out by the very thing they were here to destroy. He willed himself to stay calm and looked about properly. The inside of the tower was no bigger than a walk-in closet and it reeked of petrol fumes.

Harm was already tearing up the grass to get at the sandy soil beneath. 'Where's the valve thing?'

Adam peered around at the generator until his eyes fixed on a black plastic cowl on one side marked AIR INTAKE protected by a grille. He tapped it. 'Just like David said,' he murmured. 'But since we don't have claws, we'll need a screwdriver.'

'We've got a rock,' Harm reported, handing him a sharp stone. Hoping the generator's racket would mask the sound, he smashed it against the black grille, again and again. His efforts loosened the screws just enough for Harm to turn them with her fingers. She winced as the metal bit into her finger-tips and finally pulled the cover free.

Adam hesitated. 'How much sand do you think we'll need to zap it?'

'Just chuck in loads,' Harm decided, and poured both handfuls into the engine's cooling fan. Adam grabbed a handful and tossed it in too, as Harm went back for more. Suddenly the two of them were throwing the sand, recklessly, wildly. *Finally we're doing something back to the raptors*, Adam thought dizzily, *sticking it back to Geneflow.*

Then the generator's hum changed pitch, and a sickly whine started up beneath the unsteady tug of their breathing.

'We've done it,' Harm muttered. 'Time to go.'

'You first,' said Adam, 'I'll help push you out.'

Harm squeezed herself through the narrow gap, gasping, wriggling and shifting about, trying to make it through as quickly as possible. Adam prayed there were no raptors waiting just outside. The floodlights were still glaring as he scrambled through after her into the fresher air. He couldn't hear anything over the juddering noise. His ribs felt like they were going to crack but somehow, with Harm pulling on his arms, he made it back out – just as the lights began to flicker. Scraped and bruised, he collapsed with Harm onto the sandy grass. As he did so the generator threw a grinding, grating screech out into the night and the lights slammed off.

At once, unearthly noises rose from the dark camp – howls and hoots and hoarse mutterings. Heavy figures came crashing through the grass, seemingly from all directions.

Adam gripped tightly onto Harm's hand, hauled her up and ran with her into the jungle. As they smashed through the wild undergrowth, he wondered how they could safely rejoin the others.

He was still wondering when they ran straight into a Brute.

It was huge, claws long and lethal, the tangle of quills on its chest like countless talons reaching out to rake them. Harm yelled in alarm. The creature actually took a step backwards, surprised perhaps by this prey that had no scent. Then its tail lashed out, smashing splinters from the tree beside Adam's head. Harm yanked him away and they sprinted off in the only direction possible – back towards the Vel camp.

The ground rocked with heavy footfalls as the raptor recovered itself and gave chase. A terrible, ululating howl went up from somewhere close by. A Vel call-to-arms or Brute battle cry? Whichever, it was soon followed by the ringing of claw on metal, the whistling of air as spike-tipped tails whipped and swung, and the squawks and barks of wounded beasts, a cacophony raking apart the night.

The Brute attack is underway already, Adam realized, *and we're caught in the middle of it.*

'Those things are faster than us,' Harm panted as she and Adam ran breathlessly through the jungle murk towards the generator tower. 'Maybe if we climb up—'

But then the crocodilian head of another Brute flashed out at them from the undergrowth. Adam yelled and ducked aside, feeling its acid spray spatter the flesh of his arm. He put on a burst of speed to keep up with Harm as she raced through the long grass past the tower. But the second Brute was gaining, its jaws snapping, claws reaching out to skewer him . . .

With a shriek of defiance, a Vel hurtled out from nowhere and threw itself at the Brute invader, sickle-claws tearing at its belly. *Loner?* Adam thought with a surge of hope. But no, this was a larger, bulkier creature, unwounded — as yet. The two seven-foot reptiles smashed into a tree and half-uprooted it. Adam glanced back for a second, saw the Vel's jaws sinking into the Brute's neck even as the Brute forced its claws into the Vel's eyes, each bathing the other in blood. Then the first Brute emerged from the jungle and drove its tail like a sledgehammer into the injured Vel's skull, again and again. Barking and yowling, the two Brutes tore their foe to pieces.

Horrified, Adam turned and ran on. But where was Harm? The darkness was disorientating — everything looked different in shadow and the noise of threat and combat was growing louder, harsher.

I can't even shout her name, Adam realized, shrinking into the scant cover of some small and scrubby bushes, *I'll get us both killed, I'll—*

With a bellowing roar, a massive armoured Vel sentry thundered past Adam's hiding place. The two Brutes left the corpse of their victim at their feet and stomped towards the newcomer. The sentry backed slowly away towards the forest — as two more Vels flew out of the jungle foliage, sickle-claws slashing, jaws snapping. It had been a trap. Now it was three against two. In a blur of violence, the sentry blocked an acid strike with the armour on its arm, grabbed hold of the Brute and snapped its neck, even as his pack-brothers stabbed at it with their own claws. The other Brute refused to retreat, spitting and clawing at the Vels as they wrestled him to the ground through sheer weight of numbers.

Got to head for the outbuilding, thought Adam, *it's close to the cliffs, maybe I can climb down and hide.* He crawled for the building on all fours, sick with dread, alive with adrenaline. He realized the sky was beginning to lighten — he'd soon be easier to spot.

But then a different kind of scream rang out. Terrified. Human.

'Harm,' Adam breathed. He got to his feet and broke into a sprint before his head could even process what he was doing, following the winding power cable. *There must be something I can do*, he thought helplessly as he burst out of the undergrowth close to the now-dead electrified fence. He saw two Vel sentries lying in twisted heaps on the blood-soaked ground. He saw the door standing wide open and trampled nests inside.

And he heard a familiar cold, choking voice from the other side of the outbuilding. 'Sweet. Perfect. Mine.'

Adam crouched behind one of the reptile corpses and saw the Brute with the hunched back advancing on Harmony, who was sprawled on her back on the grass, tears in her eyes and frozen with terror. He opened his mouth to shout out, to try to distract the Brute, buy Harm time to get up and run for her life.

Then a menacing, cackling hiss stirred the hackles on his neck as a scorching jet of fluid arrowed over his shoulder past his face. An inarticulate noise escaped his lips as he realized how close he'd come to getting the back of his skull burned open. He turned to find another Brute behind him, the largest yet. Its jaws were still drooling and its dark eyes shone in the scaly, mud-brown face, which was crowned with a thick coronet of barbed wire.

The Brute queen. All other thoughts were shattered in that terrified moment of recognition. Adam tried to run but stumbled over the Vel corpse and fell.

'Adam!' Harm cried out as Hunchback turned and almost crushed him with a heavy clawed foot as it turned to face its queen.

'We want soft-skins alive.' The towering creature started towards Harm, claws clicking and catching the rising sunlight. 'Alive for the newborns' feast.'

But Hunchback barred her way, stretching its neck as if trying to match his queen for height. 'Back,' it rasped. 'The girl is perfect. Mine.'

'Bent-backed scum.' The queen tilted her head to one side and spat flecks of acid at his face, her hate-filled eyes agleam. 'I rule you.'

'No.' Jaws twitching, Hunchback shook his head. 'We do not serve you.'

Adam saw Harm, still on her back, edging side-ways on her elbows towards him. The Brute queen noticed too, swung her head towards Harm and hissed — just as Hunchback lunged forwards and stuck his claws into her flank in a series of swift, razor-like slices. 'Mine!' he barked again.

With a shout more of disbelief than of pain, the queen cuffed Hunchback hard around the jaws and grabbed him in a bearhug. She ground his throat against the fierce thorns of her chest-quills, opening the flesh in twenty places. Hunchback thrashed and flailed, blood and acid frothing in its throat.

Harm stared as though rooted to the spot. 'Quick,' Adam panted, grabbing her wrist and pulling her to her feet. 'While they're distracted.' But he hesitated himself – should they run for the cliff edge and hope they could climb down out of reach, or run back into the jungle?

Even as the thoughts flashed through his mind, the Brute queen finished with Hunchback. Once his body flopped at her feet and lay still, she looked up, licked her bloody claws and fixed Harm and Adam with her hate-filled stare.

'Now!' Adam insisted, breaking into a sprint for the jungle treeline and dragging Harm along with him.

'We can't outrun that thing,' she shouted.

'We have to,' snapped Adam.

The Brute queen was already coming for them.

Harm broke free of Adam's grip and began to climb the nearest tree, legs and arms at ninety degrees to the trunk, scaling it as swiftly as Adam might've climbed the stairs. As the huge beast quickened its stride Adam tried to climb up after her, but his own technique was clumsy in comparison. The giant reptile was closing the distance between them with terrifying speed.

'Come on,' Harm shouted down at him. 'Do it!'

Adam half-climbed, half-shinned his way up the rough trunk, adrenaline giving him strength he'd never known. The pounding footfalls grew louder. Then the Brute queen slammed into the tree with colossal force. The sturdy trunk shook. Adam clung on with all his strength as he felt himself begin to slip. The Brute bellowed, scoring the tree with her lethal claws. Harm reached out to pull Adam higher. His fingers touched hers, then slipped free as the Brute queen kicked and shook the base of the tree, rasping and bellowing with fury, pawing the sandy ground as she heaved her weight against the wood. A deep, creaking, splitting noise made Adam stare down. He saw the tree roots rising to the surface, shifting like immense tendons in a convulsing arm.

The tree was beginning to upend.

Harm shrieked as the beast shook the trunk harder and Adam finally lost his grip, plunging to the ground . . .

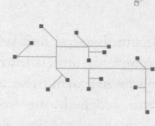

17: Not Alone

As Adam struck the ground hard on his shoulder and lay winded, a blur of red and black scales launched itself from the jungle gloom and smashed into the Brute queen.

'Loner!' Harm shouted.

Adam raised his head, stunned by his sudden rescue. He watched spellbound as Loner pounced on the fallen Brute and slashed at her throat with his claws, his bad arm apparently healed. *He's back risking his life for us. We're still in with a shot.* But the queen fought back viciously, scoring deep slashes in Loner's shoulder and kicking him away. Loner fell back gasping, bobbed his head as though bowing and turned down his claws – a submissive gesture, an appeal for mercy. *Mercy that he's not going to get*, thought Adam helplessly, as the bloodied Brute queen stomped forwards and raised her lethal foot claw to open Loner's belly.

But before she could move, she was engulfed in a storm of blue light, like vicious lightning playing all around her. The Brute shrieked and wailed, falling to her knees as a scorched, static smell filled the air. With a chill Adam saw two men in hazard suits and gas masks had emerged from his earlier hiding place, firing sophisticated electro-shock guns.

Geneflow guards, he thought numbly. *The fighting's smoked them out.*

Loner was caught up in the flashing blue vortex, joining the Brute queen in a macabre, jerking dance. Loner collapsed and the queen soon followed. Once she'd slumped to the ground, the guards stopped firing and one of them ran into the outbuilding.

'Get out of that tree.' The remaining guard trained his gun on Harm. 'Sit beside your friend.'

Harm dropped down and Adam could see she was trembling. He looked at Loner's mud-caked face; the reptile's eyes were shut, but he was still breathing. *Wake up*, Adam willed him. *Wake up!*

The one that stayed outside covered Adam and Harm with his weapon. 'Doctor Haskins, there's a couple of kids here,' he called to his friend. 'Live ones.'

'Deal with them, J.J.,' Haskins called from inside the outbuilding. 'There's just one egg I can see here that might still be viable . . .' The man came outside holding a large plastic case; Adam could see the football-sized egg nestling inside. 'Double check I didn't miss anything. I've got to get this back to the lab before the surviving Utahraptors take over . . .'

He hurried away and J.J. shrugged at Harm and Adam. 'Sorry, kids. But trust me, you won't want to know much about it when these things hold their feast . . .'

Adam looked helplessly at Harm. She had already closed her eyes in grim anticipation. *You have to wake up, Loner*, he thought again. *Wake up!* 'Loner!'

At the cry of his name, the raptor's eyes snapped open. Before J.J. could react, Loner launched himself through the air, pushing off with his tail as well as his hind legs in an awesome pounce at the guard. A gush of blue sparks poured from the shock-gun's nozzle, catching him in mid-air. Loner twisted his long neck and butted J.J. in the face, knocking him back into the fence so hard that it broke under his weight. The gun dropped from the guard's hand, and Adam raced over to grab it.

'Adam!' Chen burst from the jungle, his face streaked with sweat and dirt. Lisa, David and Dr Stone were huddled close behind him. 'You OK?'

Adam wanted to sink to his knees with relief at the sight of them. 'Not really,' he said hoarsely, and crawled over to where Loner lay. 'Thank you,' he whispered.

Loner looked at him, his eyes alight, and nodded.

'Your pet raptor said he could hear you,' Chen went on. 'Charged off like a dog chasing a postman.'

'We couldn't get here any sooner, honey.' Lisa helped Harm up and hugged her. 'There were so many Brutes in the jungle, surrounding the camp.'

David nodded, eyeing the dead Hunchback and the body of the Brute queen warily. 'The Vels fought the first wave back, and when the Brutes fled into the trees they followed – straight into an ambush.'

'I thought we were all dead,' Stone muttered, scratches vivid on his deathly pale face.

'If you'd got here sooner you probably would've been.' Harm pointed to the outbuilding and looked straight at Chen. 'Good place to meet – under guard and full of Vel eggs.'

Lisa's hand flew to her mouth and David put a comforting arm around her. 'Eggs?'

Chen swore under his breath. The shock on his face seemed genuine.

'The Brutes have smashed most of them,' Adam told him. 'But these two guards came with weapons and took down the queen, and one of them took an egg he thought might be all right . . .'

Lisa looked closely at the man in the hazard suit sprawled in the wreck of the fence. 'This guy's from Geneflow. That's one of the roaches that killed Andy.'

Dr Stone hurried forward. 'He's badly hurt.'

'Good,' said David fiercely.

'We want to get into their base, don't we?' Chen reminded him. 'This jerk can help us.'

'Like, a hostage?' Harm said.

'The guy's called J.J.,' Adam murmured. 'He almost killed Harm and me. If Loner hadn't saved us when he did . . .'

'It's not safe to wait here.' David crossed to join them and took the electro-shock gun from Adam. 'The fighting's still going on.'

Adam nodded. 'And any Vels will come and try to save their eggs.'

'No.' Loner shook his head weakly. 'They will smell . . . the eggs are smashed.'

'Well, the Brutes are going to smell their dead queen for sure,' said Harm. 'And they're going to come looking.'

'She is not dead. Only wounded.' Loner got up, loped over to the gargantuan body, staring down at it. Then with a hiss he brought his hooked claws down on the back of the queen's neck. Adam grimaced as he pulled them back out, dripping with gore. 'Now, she is dead.' Loner plucked the barbed-wire coronet from the grey, misshapen head, and crushed it in his fist.

Though his stomach turned, Adam couldn't help feeling a sense of relief — relief that almost outweighed his unease at Loner's sudden violence. *He's still an animal at the end of the day*, he reminded himself. *It's no different from a lion or tiger killing a rival.*

He's just better equipped to kill than most anything on earth, that's all.

Chen barely seemed to have noticed a thing, crouching over the guard's body. 'Come on, J.J. While it's all quiet, you've got some talking to do . . .' He tried to pull the man into a sitting position – but as he did, a scraping noise was accompanied by a rush of blood from the back of the man's shoulder. 'Doc! Get over here.'

Adam grimaced as he saw a splintered fence post jutting from the grass, soaked crimson. 'He must've fallen onto it.'

Stone hurried over with his bag. 'Help me get this suit off him.'

Chen pulled off the helmet, unmasking a round-faced man with dark skin, a shaved head and a bloodied, broken nose. Loner loomed over him, and Adam watched anxiously as he stretched out with those bloody claws. But with scalpel precision the raptor only tore open the rubbery neckline of the hazard suit and the white T-shirt beneath it before stepping back. Stone regarded the raptor for a moment before carefully peeling away the clothing to uncover an ugly wound.

'My arm,' J.J. gasped, coming round. 'What . . . what did I do?'

'You messed up, J.J.' Chen smiled at him. 'Now, it looks like you need a doctor. I got one right here but first you need to tell us a few things.'

J.J. looked pale and sweaty. His T-shirt was soaked with blood. Loner seemed transfixed, drool frothing in his jaws, claws twitching. Adam realized the raptor must be ravenous, and here was helpless prey sat right in front of him.

'Get that thing away from me,' the guard hissed. 'I don't know how you're controlling it, but—'

'Who says we *are* controlling it?' sneered Lisa.

'Speak to me, J.J.,' said Chen casually. 'Or we let the raptor speak to you, and he doesn't talk so nice.'

The guard's eyes hardened. 'I'm telling you nothing.'

'Well, I'm telling *you* that you have an anterior dislocation of the shoulder, possibly with a fracture of the proximal end of the humerus,' said Stone. 'And this puncture wound may have caused a partial rupture of the axillary artery.' He mustered a grave smile. 'It's what we doctors call "a mess". Right now, your body's pumped full of endorphins to reduce the pain and shock, but pretty soon you're going to be hurting big time. And if I don't stop the bleeding you're a dead man.'

Chen leaned in closer. 'Sure you won't think again, buddy?'

'All right,' J.J. muttered finally, sweat pouring over his bloody face. 'But I don't know much. I'm hired help. Private security expert.'

'A mercenary,' David translated, looking down at the gun in his hands. 'Soldier for hire.'

'I only got here three weeks ago, relieving some other guy. Please, you've got to pop my shoulder . . .' Stone reached round, took the man's wrist and bent his arm into an L-shape.

'Wait.' Harm was suspicious at once. 'The sea monsters trash any ship that comes close. We've seen them.'

'Up close,' Chen added. 'So how did you get past them?'

When the guard didn't respond, Chen put a hand on Stone's arm to stop him fixing the dislocation. 'I'll ask you one more time.'

J.J. spoke through gritted teeth. 'A woman called Josephs controls them somehow. Computers and stuff.'

Stone rotated the man's arm outwards, popping the shoulder back into its joint. J.J. gasped, then shook as if with intense relief. But blood was still pooling from the wound and Stone began tying a tourniquet around the top of J.J.'s arm.

'Think-Send,' Adam breathed, and leaned closer to the guard. 'You said computers — does someone put on a headset linked to a kind of metal box when they tell the monsters what to do?'

J.J. stared. 'How would a kid like you know . . . ?' He trailed off, clamming up.

I'll take that as a yes, thought Adam, pleased with himself.

As Stone took a big wad of gauze and started taping it over the wound, Harm spoke up. 'Did Geneflow use this Think-Send to put thoughts from the Death Row prisoners' heads into the raptors?'

J.J. looked at her blankly.

Even Adam wondered what she was talking about.

'We need to get out of here,' said David before Harm could explain. 'Anti-stink spray or not, Vels and Brutes alike will be able to smell that man's blood.'

'At least we've got a gun that works against the raptors now.' Chen carefully avoided Loner's gaze as he turned back to Adam. 'You understand this Think-Send stuff, right?'

Finally, thought Adam, *something I can feel confident about*. 'I've used it more than anyone. If we can find the computer and the program I can switch off those things that trashed the *Hula Queen*.'

'Yes,' Loner wheezed. 'Stop them. You must.'

David nodded eagerly. 'If we could contact your other ship, bring it back here . . .'

'We could all get away.' Lisa clutched Harm to her. 'Far away from here.'

Dad, thought Adam, hope charging through him. *I could see Dad again . . .*

Then a roaring howl grated out from the jungle, and the sound of something smashing through the vegetation. Despite the morning sun, Adam felt the temperature drop by degrees.

'Prehistoric fight club's back,' said Chen. He started pulling the remains of the hazard suit from J.J.'s battered body. 'Tell me, how many people does Geneflow have here?'

'Skeleton staff,' J.J. muttered. 'Josephs, two other science-types, three guards and me.'

David looked at Chen. 'If we can set free the prisoners we'd have strength of numbers on our side.'

'Those poor saps are weaker than you are,' J.J. retorted, wincing as Stone wrapped the tape tightly up and around his neck. 'Anyway, they're locked up.'

Chen turned to David, Stone and Lisa and started pulling on the torn hazard suit. 'Keep our new friend behind you. I'll walk in front – if we meet anyone, from a distance they'll think I'm him.' He raised the electro-shock gun. 'At least until I can zap them.'

As they set off cautiously across the camp, Adam

fell into weary step beside Harm. Distant cries and yowls coloured the rainforest gloom. The Brutes were calling to each other. Communicating instructions, screeching understanding. The racket creeped Adam out big-time.

Turning to Harm, he decided to work on his own communication. 'Why were you asking about Think-Send and the prisoners?'

Harm shrugged. 'It's nothing. Forget it.'

'That raptor with the hunched back,' Adam persisted. 'Was it what he said to you?'

Harm hesitated. 'It's too weird,' she said, the words falling out in a rush as if trying to escape before she could change her mind. 'The hunchback was in that supersized chicken coop, smashing up stuff, and I saw it was him and I tried to run past but he saw me and came running out and I fell . . .' She bit her lip, put on the brakes. 'I guess you heard what he called me.'

Adam nodded. 'Like before. Sweet. Perfect . . .'

'Yeah.' She snorted softly. 'What got to me was that it's sort of what my dad used to say to me. ''Cause of my name, get it? Sing in sweet harmony, perfect harmony, yada yada yada . . .' She shook her head. 'It's nothing.'

Adam considered. 'Well, you know, Think-Send has transmitted some of my thoughts by accident before. If the convicts used the system to play games and the same sets were used to train the raptors, I suppose it's possible . . .'

'. . . That I'm clutching at straws. I get it, it's OK. You don't have to be nice.' Harm shrugged. 'I guess that freak with the back just wanted feeding, is all. I mean, just look at all this meat on my bones.' She looked at him wryly. 'Who wouldn't think I was perfect?'

Not sure what to say, Adam could feel himself blushing. But as they passed the tower he could feel the colour drain from his cheeks. The path to the main entrance was strewn with raptor corpses; Vels and Brutes locked in combat even in death. The barricade and the main entrance had been torn apart, the piles of scrap lying like strange headstones around the killing ground. Adam saw Loner looking all around, his eyes unreadable.

'Can you scent if any of the Vels are still alive?' Adam asked.

'I am the last.' There was no emotion in his voice. He smelled the air. 'Brutes have been inside. They are not there now.'

'You can't scent the guards, though, can you,' said Chen, 'and they could be laying on something special for us. I'd better check it out.' He moved towards the shadowed entrance. 'You've got the raptor to look out for you till I get back. Stay here.'

'Like there's anywhere else to go.' Harm

crouched beside an overturned packing crate, and David gestured the others to join her in hiding amid the remains of the barricade as Chen cautiously approached the ruined entrance. Adam sank down behind a rusted up generator, mindful that the one he'd helped destroy had brought this bloody massacre down on the camp.

More crashes carried from the jungle. 'The Brutes who made it are coming back,' J.J. promised them. 'Saw them on the spy-cams, shifting their eggs from the beach.'

'Taking the enemies' territory,' Stone noted.

J.J. shrugged. 'The prisoners are in no state to make the trek to the beach. Easier to bring the eggs here for their feast.'

'You're so cold about it.' Lisa glared at him. 'Have you been spying on us too down in your safe little base? Laughing at us?'

'Get over yourself,' sneered the guard. 'The spy-cams come built into key raptors on each side. It's them Josephs watches. You're nothing.'

Suddenly a Brute crashed out of the jungle gloom and into the clearing – three large, pale eggs clamped in its claws. Adam slid down further behind his rusted metal cover, and the others followed suit. But Loner was too big to hide himself.

The Brute saw him at once. It threw back its head and screamed, a terrible, gargling summons to its pack, and the hate in its eyes was as eloquent as its howl.

There's a Vel left standing. Who cares what it did for us? Tear it apart.

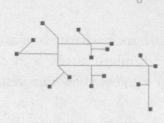

18. Outside In

Loner grabbed a rusted sheet of corrugated iron for a shield and charged at the Brute. It wasted barely a second as it stooped to place its eggs on the ground.

But that was long enough for Loner to close the distance between them.

He slammed the scrap metal against the Brute's body, knocking it to the ground. Its writhing tail shattered one of the eggs, and Loner stamped on the other two with a savage hiss of satisfaction before running back to the barricade, a blur of red and black — just as three more battle-scarred Brutes came out of the jungle, barking and roaring.

'Where's Chen?' David whispered, staring in horror as the Brutes advanced. 'Why hasn't he come back — what's waiting for us in there?'

Stone took hold of J.J.'s good arm. 'At least we have a hostage.'

'Inside,' Loner rasped to the humans around him.

David pushed J.J. through the entrance. 'C'mon,

kids,' said Lisa. She took Harm and Adam by the hand and started hauling them into the wartime building that now served as the Vel camp. The entrance hall was dingy and damp, poorly lit through high and broken windows. It stank like a zoo enclosure, only twenty times stronger.

Adam snatched his hand from Lisa's grip. 'I'll catch you up,' he called, and ran back to the doorway. The Brutes were advancing steadily. 'Loner, please, come on.'

'Your queen is dead,' the Vel bellowed at his enemies, holding up the mangled band of barbed wire their leader had once worn. 'I killed her.'

The words had a varied effect on the Brutes. Some growled, some sniffed the air, others barked and yelped like dogs or wolves. He could see two of Loner's allies – the one-eyed Brute and its friend with the broken teeth – hanging back at the jungle's edge, impassive.

The Brute that Loner had knocked down kicked away the corrugated iron and got back to its feet. It stared down at the broken, stinking eggs at his feet. 'I will kill you,' it croaked.

'No.' Another shook its huge head. '*I* will kill the Vel.'

'Who among you is strong enough to wear this crown?' Loner bit through the circlet of barbed wire to Brute yowls of anger, then hurled it out into the clearing. The creatures fell upon the token, snapping and slashing at each other to get a hold of it.

'Now.' Loner turned and snatched Adam away, holding him around the waist like a fullback running the ball up-field, and darted into the building.

'Cool distraction,' Adam gasped as Loner's quill-points bit into his skin, his pounding footfalls echoing the thump of Adam's heart. 'I can't believe they're so stupid they'd fight among themselves before they come to get us.'

Loner looked down at him as they ran, and Adam could've sworn he was smiling. 'Stupidity is good.'

Maybe, Adam thought. *But when they've sorted that little spat, the Brutes will really be out for blood.*

Like they weren't already.

Lisa, David, Harm and Stone were waiting for them at a junction between two corridors. J.J. was leaning against the stained concrete, pale and sweating. Loner put Adam down beside them with surprising gentleness.

'He was brilliant.' Adam smiled nervously at the raptor. 'Bought us some time.'

Lisa pressed a hand against Loner's side. 'Bless you.'

'Uh-huh, God bless the talking dinosaur.' Stone looked around distractedly. 'Where's John? We need him, where is he?'

'My people must have got him,' said J.J., starting off uncertainly down the corridor to the left. 'Let's go.'

David held him back. 'So Geneflow can kill us too, like they killed the people we loved?'

'I won't let them hurt you,' J.J. promised. 'You helped me, I help you, right?'

Lisa chewed her lip. 'Maybe he means it—'

'We can't trust him,' Stone insisted.

The concrete floor carried the vibration as heavy clawed feet pounded in the distance. 'The Brutes will kill us all if we stay here,' hissed J.J.

'The armoury,' Loner said. 'The Vels kept human weapons . . .'

'From the Second World War.' David nodded. 'Like the tear gas they used on us at the dugout.'

'The armoury is on the way to the hidden door,' Loner said, as the stamping steps drew closer. He curled his tail urgently as though beckoning the humans to follow, guiding them through the twists and turns of the base. David and Lisa went first while Adam ran with Harm, his legs feeling leaden, praying they didn't have much further to go. He turned to ask J.J. – just as the guard stumbled and fell to the ground.

Stone, already out of breath, dropped to examine him. 'He's out. Lost too much blood.'

While Loner and Harm ran on ahead, Adam

hesitated. And before David could stop Lisa she had run back to Stone and J.J. 'We'll have to carry him,' she said.

A hunting roar echoed hard off the concrete. The Brutes weren't far off.

'There's no time, Lisa,' David argued. 'Those things will smell his blood and get straight on our trail.'

'We can't just leave him here,' Lisa insisted, as she and Stone struggled to lift the big man. 'Whatever he's done.'

David marched back to her, grabbed her arm. 'Please, Lisa—'

'Someone loves this man, just like you loved your sister and I loved Andy.' Lisa took J.J.'s feet as Stone lifted him under his arms. 'I'm not leaving anyone to die.'

David shook his head but he helped them anyway. 'I guess neither am I,' he muttered. 'Least of all you.'

'Quickly!' Harm hissed from along the corridor, and Adam ran on to join her. Loner stood in front of a metal doorway, his claws raking through rust as he tried to prise it open. At his feet was the body of a Vel in a thick pool of blood, two bands of orange material wrapped around its right arm. Adam looked at Harm. 'Did Loner . . . ?'

'No. It was already dead,' Harm informed him. 'Sides split open.'

'Leader of the Council of Blood,' Loner grunted.

'Must've been trying to get to the weapons,' Adam supposed.

'Come *on*, Loner,' Harm urged him. Lisa, David and Stone came up with J.J. and set him down, catching their breaths. Growling carried eerily through the corridors.

And then Adam heard a scuffling further down the passage. It didn't sound big enough to be a dinosaur. He edged closer – there looked to be a single door at the end of the corridor, debris that might once've been a barricade scattered before it. It was closed, but muffled voices still carried.

'What is it?' Harm had come to join him.

'Not sure,' Adam admitted. 'But this must be the way into the Geneflow base, which means it's the sick bay. Maybe Loner was wrong about all the Vels being dead, maybe some were injur—'

There was a colossal explosion!

Adam and Harm were thrown through the air. Adam cracked his head on the concrete and lay reeling as the world seemed to spin in scarlet clashes of sound and vision. He felt Harm's hand on his pulling him up, heard her shout: 'Lisa! David!'

At least I can still hear this time, thought Adam. Smoke was pouring from the armoury, and dust and plaster were raining down from the roof.

Loner staggered out, bloody welts rising all over

his battered body. 'Door,' he breathed. 'Booby-trapped. Stop intruders getting hold of the weapons.'

'Harm?' Lisa's voice sounded through the roiling smoke. 'Adam, honey?'

'We're OK!' Harm started forwards.

But then a Brute loomed out of the smoke, teeth bared. One of its arms looked withered, like the one back at the bone pit.

'Lisa!' Harm yelled. 'David!' But she was answered with shouts aimed somewhere else.

'Get away!' Lisa's scream hurt Adam's ears. 'No!'

'Get off her!' Stone yelled.

Then the human voices were drowned out by the Brute's hungry shriek. Loner turned and grabbed Adam and Harm, carrying them towards the sick bay. 'No!' Harm sobbed. 'They can't . . . can't be—'

Another Brute pushed through the swirling cloud. It was a giant, its powerful body raked with battle-scars – and the barbed-wire coronet of rule was clutched in its claws. Adam flinched as it bellowed and stamped after them. *Please let us get away*, was all Adam could think. *Please, if there's anyone listening . . .*

Someone was. As they reached the door at the end of the passage it flew open – to reveal Agent John Chen. He looked bruised and shaken and was fighting for breath.

Loner let Adam and Harm go and Chen tossed Adam a shock-gun. 'Catch.' He pressed another into Harm's hands. Adam stared dumbly at the weapon for a moment, then raised it and pulled the trigger. The gun almost shook itself out of his grip as coruscating blue sparks arced along the passage, catching the pursuing Brute in mid-stride. Chen fired too, and finally Harm. The beast slumped to its knees, jerking and shaking in the cobalt-blue haze before finally collapsing.

'Now we get Lisa and the others.' Harm started forwards but three more of the nightmarish monsters stamped into sight. Loner ducked inside the sick bay as Chen fired again, Adam and Harm joining in a beat later. But since they were no longer concentrating their fire, the Brutes were forcing their way forwards, slowly gaining ground, roaring and barking their defiance.

'No good,' Chen shook his head. 'We can't stop them.'

Harm kept on firing. 'But Lisa and David are out there,' she shouted. 'Your friend Stone—'

'Getting ourselves killed won't help them,' Chen told her. 'What's keeping your pet raptor? Adam, go chase him up!'

While Chen and Harm kept firing, Adam went into the darkened sick bay. It stank – the ripe, pungent smell of muck and decay. There were two long-dead Vels, curled up in a heap, and two human guards slumped over their remains. Loner turned round quickly, almost guiltily, as Adam entered, his back flat to the wall as a hidden door in the mouldering breezeblocks slid open.

'You *did* it!' Adam stared at the modern, redbrick walls beyond, and he almost threw himself inside to the safety it promised. 'Agent Chen, Harm,' he shouted, 'Loner did it! He's got the door open into the Geneflow base.'

Chen charged in, dragging Harm behind him, to roars of triumph from the Brutes in the corridor. 'Move,' he ordered Adam, bundling him and Harm through the door. Only once they were all inside did Loner follow. He slammed his tail against a large black button in the wall. The concrete-clad door slid soundlessly shut. A steel shutter hummed down from above, sealing the entrance completely. Built into it was a plasma screen that had to be linked to some hidden spy-cam, giving a virtual view of the room beyond, as two Brutes slammed their way inside. They kicked at the bodies on the floor, staring round in agitation, teeth bared and acid dribbling from their jaws.

Harm leaned against a wall and sank down it slowly, her bony brown legs folding under her, her eyes tightly shut. Adam wanted to say something comforting but nothing came to mind. He released a long shuddering breath he didn't know he'd been holding.

Loner padded across the room stealthily to the far door. 'I must remind myself . . . where to go. Check it's safe.' His claws scraped against the metal handle as he pushed it open. Then he moved quietly down a flight of crude concrete steps.

No hanging around, thought Adam. His head was throbbing where he'd knocked it in the explosion, his ears were still ringing and he felt sick with nerves and fatigue – and at the thought of what had happened to Lisa, David and Stone outside. *If they hadn't stopped to help J.J. they might have been closer to us when the booby trap went off and we'd all have escaped in here together . . .*

Yeah. *If.*

Chen was studying the coloured wires connecting to the screen in the shutter. 'The camera on the other side of that door feeds straight into here. It's like a spy-hole in the door, not routed through to any main security.'

'Makes sense,' said Adam. 'Loner got in and out through it lots of times.'

'Should mean we're safe here for a little while.' Chen's eyes flicked about the antechamber as he thought things through out loud. 'Two guards in there, like J.J. – either dead or out of the way. If he wasn't snowing us, that leaves one more in here someplace; most likely Josephs' personal minder, looking after her and her scientist buddies . . .'

'I think it was a scientist who took a Vel egg back here,' Adam said, trying to catch his breath. 'They're most likely tied up now, studying it.'

'Makes sense,' Chen agreed. 'They wouldn't be expecting a bunch of prehistoric animals to be real good with hidden entry coders . . .'

'Where *were* you?' Harm spoke at last, trembling with rage as she glared up at Chen. 'If you hadn't left us waiting so long, we wouldn't have had to run from those Brutes, J.J. wouldn't have passed out, Lisa and David—'

Chen held up a hand. 'You can yell at me all you want once I've got the facts straight. Adam, what was that explosion?'

'The armoury was booby-trapped,' Adam said. 'Some kind of bomb. Loner was trying to get weapons to fight off the Brutes.'

'And what about Doc Stone?'

'I heard him call out.'

'David and Lisa called out too,' Harm said quietly.

Chen nodded. 'I don't think those things will kill them. Not yet.' He looked at Harm, his breath was coming hard, his eyes haunted. 'See, the reason I left you waiting was because . . . I found the other survivors.'

Adam swallowed. 'You did?'

'Maybe thirty of them.' Chen looked haunted. 'They're thin as sticks but still alive. I tried to get them out of this stinking hole they're shut up in, some old officers' mess or something. But I couldn't. Two of Josephs' guards caught me, started dragging me in here. When that explosion went off it gave me the distraction I needed to deal with them.'

Adam saw the Brutes still rampaging on the screen. 'They've been dealt with now, all right.'

Chen shook his head wearily. 'I'm sorry. You're just a kid; you shouldn't have to be seeing this stuff. Some Christmas, huh . . .' He started pacing the room. 'I'm sorry I got you messed up in everything. Truly, I am. This was meant to be my fight – a fight I never really planned on walking away from.' He looked at Adam beseechingly. 'I mean, d'you think I would've kidnapped you and your dad if I was expecting to go back to the office Monday and face the consequences? I'm already under investigation, I'll most likely go to jail. I came here 'cause I got nothing left to lose . . .' He slammed his fist against the wall. 'So how come I'm still here and my last friends are lying dead on this island, huh? How'd things work out this way—?'

'Oh, don't you *dare* start feeling sorry for yourself.' Harm jumped up, her eyes dark and blazing.

'Don't you dare. At least this was your choice. The rest of us . . .'

The words choked off. But she refused to cry. Adam laid a hand on her wrist. She didn't move it.

Suddenly the door to the stairwell squeaked and banged open. Chen whirled round, raised his electro-shock gun. But it was only Loner, eyes bright in his scorched, muddy face. 'Come with me,' he hissed.

Aching but alert, Adam, Harm and Chen followed the huge reptile to the top of the dingy stairwell. There was a lift, but Loner took the long flight of stairs down into the gloom. Chen and Harm followed first, their footsteps echoing and re-echoing against the bare rock walls.

Adam took a deep breath and went after them. Just barely out of the frying pan, it was already time to descend into the fire.

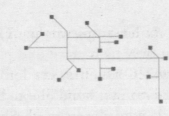

19: Alta-Vita

It seemed the staircase would never end. What kind of a job must it have been, Adam wondered, excavating the cliff-face beneath the old military base so Geneflow could work and plot safely off the world's radar?

Like rats in a hole, thought Adam. And as he and Harm followed Chen and Loner deeper and deeper, he couldn't think of a less likely group of exterminators.

'Doesn't look like they ever finished this place,' Harm remarked.

'They saved their money for their whole weird science thing,' said Adam.

'Let's hope they didn't waste much money on CCTV,' Chen muttered.

'In here,' said Loner, as they finally reached another level. A short corridor extended left off the stairwell, leading to another elevator and a set of large double doors. Chen opened them up, to reveal a vast storeroom, lined with shelves and littered with crates and boxes and half-empty cartons.

Harm stared round suspiciously. 'This has to mean . . .' She ran over to a crate and pulled out a huge bag of crisps. 'Oh, my sweet lord.' She tore open the bag and shoved a handful into her mouth. Tears began to roll down her cheeks. She grinned, tried to speak again but it only came out as chip shrapnel. Adam ran over but stopped as he saw a rack of two-litre bottles of purified water. It felt as though he'd just found a chest of solid gold. He waved a bottle at Harm, who barrelled over and snatched it from him, tearing off the lid, swigging deeply. There were dozens more bottles. Chen took one, Adam opened another and gulped greedily, almost choking. Then he tasted the salty crisps, and it was like crunching through heaven.

Chen threw a bottle to Loner, who sliced the top off and emptied it down his scaly throat in seconds. Adam gave him another bottle and then found a huge catering tin of chicken soup, which Loner tore open and lapped at hungrily.

'Three months,' Harm muttered. She'd moved on to a tin of pasta in tomato sauce, emptying it into her mouth and spilling most down her top. 'Three months of starving and thirsting . . .' She wiped her mouth and licked her fingers, still laughing and crying. 'Oh, David, Lisa, why couldn't you be here for this?'

With the initial euphoria of finding fresh supplies

fading a little, Adam could feel his stomach turn at the thought of what would come next. He wished he hadn't eaten so quickly.

'Check this.' Chen swigged from his bottle again and pointed to a diagram on the wall. 'Looks like a map of the place, back when it was a playpen for the Death Row cons.'

'Three levels underground,' said Adam.

'I'd never dreamed the place was so big,' Harm admitted.

'Half of it below sea level by the look of it.' Chen pointed to a smaller block on the lowest level adjacent to a long passageway that extended off the plan. 'Yeah, they've got their own hydro-power station here — using tidal energy to generate the electricity.'

'I'm happy for them.' Harm drank more water. 'What's that next to the power station, a tunnel?'

'It leads to a cave system,' Loner announced, his voice sounding louder and colder still in the confined space. 'One that stretches for miles. One tunnel leads to a concealed entrance close to the Brute camp.'

Adam nodded. 'I suppose that would make sense. If Josephs and her team are studying both tribes, they'd need easy access to both camps.'

'But if the Brutes are moving into the Vel camp, the beach will be safe,' Harm realized. 'If we could only get David and Lisa and everyone else out . . .'

'If we want to get off Raptor Island, we have to find the Think-Send system and try to turn off those sea monster things,' Adam reminded her. 'And contact your boat, Agent Chen. And send another email to Marrs warning him what's happening . . .'

'Plus we *have* to find Josephs,' Chen added.

'Is that all?' Harm muttered.

'I believe . . . we must descend to the lowest level.' Loner ran across in that loping, bird-like gait to join them beside the map. 'Food stores are here on the first level below ground, the laboratories are on the second level. And on the *third* level . . .' He reached out with a claw to a number of adjoining rectangles. One of them read *A-V Unit*.

'Audio-visual?' Chen wondered.

'Or Alta-Vita,' breathed Adam. 'The name of that Geneflow project you found—'

'The project that made me.' Loner tore his claw across the map, tearing the paper. 'I shall lead the way.'

Adam watched him pad back across the storeroom to the doors, and followed along with Harm and Chen, back out onto the stairwell. Then Loner stopped, his ear cocked.

The elevator was in use. Going up.

'Maybe someone's grown tired of waiting for

those guards to fetch me,' Chen murmured. 'They're coming to investigate.'

'Come on, then,' said Adam.

Loner again led the way down the stairs, his claws clacking on the concrete steps as he took them four at a time, the others hurrying close behind until they reached the bottom floor of the complex.

It was dark and deserted, musty and cold. Lights in the ceiling flickered on as they passed. The silence was all pervading, broken only by their nervous footfalls and uneven breaths. The main lab – where Adam imagined Josephs must spend most of her time – was somewhere up above, but he was convinced they would run into her at any moment, or her guards, or . . .

That's not helping. Come on, clear your head. He knew he'd need all his concentration to go straight into using Think-Send in a completely foreign program, but it was impossible not to feel that danger lurked in every shadowy corner.

Loner led them through stuffy, half-lit corridors and communal areas built for the inmates who had lost their lives to Geneflow's experiments. He seemed confined, too big for a place built with humans in mind. At one point he paused beside a row of tall, metal lockers – the kind you might find at a swimming pool or gym – and tugged open one of the doors to reveal an orange jumpsuit.

'Prison uniform,' Harm murmured.

Loner touched the fabric cautiously, almost wonderingly. Then he tore it from the hanger and threw it to the floor.

'What's wrong?' Adam asked.

'It is nothing.' Loner snorted softly. 'We have almost reached the A-V Unit.'

Chen had moved on to yet another closed door. 'Where does this lead?'

'Records are kept there,' Loner hissed. 'The place where I learned about Geneflow.' He paused. 'A computer I used to speak to Doctor Marrs. And leading on to the Alta-Vita Unit.'

'You sure did your homework on this place,' Harm observed.

Loner lowered his head. 'I was here . . . many times.'

'So, what're we waiting for?' Chen pushed at the door. It was unlocked.

Adam and Harm followed him through into a large, ragtag space where different media collided messily. Shelves and tables full of leather-bound books and journals sat alongside all kinds of weird stuff – things called ZIP drives and JAZ drives and even reels of tape, as well as CDs and huge, old-fashioned floppy disks.

There must be masses of evidence against Geneflow here, thought Adam. *Plans. Timelines. Membership lists . . .*

'That computer,' Loner rasped, pointing to the far corner of the room. 'I sent mail from there.'

Chen hurried to the PC.

Adam's attention was taken by some data disks branded MINDCORP. 'This is the company my dad worked for in New York,' he said. 'Making the most super-accurate computer model of the human brain in existence . . .'

'Another high-tech business Josephs was stealing secrets from,' Chen noted.

'But why?' murmured Adam.

'Hey, look.' Harm read the spine of a black binder leaning on a shelf. '"Inmate Files". My dad will be in here somewhere. And Andy, and David's sister . . .'

'All of these are inmate files,' Adam realized, scrutinizing a long line of binders. He picked one up and flicked through, but it was all charts and equations and in-depth psychological profiles, way over his head.

Chen took another and browsed it listlessly. 'Whatever they brought them here for, it wasn't just to be turned into raptor food.'

Adam looked at Harm. 'Maybe you were right about the convicts putting thoughts into Think-Send, to be given to the raptors later on.'

'Guess the answers'll be here some place.' Harm turned a page of a file without enthusiasm. 'But do we want to know them?'

'Exactly my business in coming here,' said Chen.

Adam nodded. 'To beat Geneflow, we have to know what they're doing.'

'We gotta write to old Marrs first. Even if Geneflow catch us they can't haul back an email. I should be able to route a message through to the *Pahalu* while I'm at it, if Rich hasn't lost his satellite phone . . .' Chen started searching through applications on the PC. 'Adam, get your butt down to this A-V Unit and start think-sending those guard dog monsters to the bottom of the sea where they can't hurt nobody. Then you and Harm can take some files out through the tunnel to Brute Beach and wait for me to get back from talking with Josephs.'

'You said . . .' Adam hesitated. 'You said you weren't counting on coming back.'

'I'm not checking out while Doc Stone might still be alive up above,' Chen assured him. 'Go on. Go.'

Adam turned to Loner. 'Will you come with me?'

'I'll go too,' said Harm.

Wordlessly the raptor padded off down the corridor to a dull green fire door. It wasn't marked 'Alta-Vita' in any way. A sign proclaimed it a GAMES ROOM.

Adam was seized by a moment's disquiet. 'I knew things were going too easily.'

'Sure this is the right place, Loner?' Harm asked.

Impatiently, Loner pushed roughly at the door.

The room inside was dark and spacious, the light that spilled in from the corridor falling far short of its corners. Adam's eyes tried to make sense of the repeated shadows he saw, and then Loner reached up and hit the light switch.

Fluorescents flickered on to reveal row after row of wooden chairs and desks, the kind you might find in an old classroom. Except, on every desk there was a sleek black console connected to a metal headset by several wires. The headsets were crudely made, with chips and circuit boards soldered to the outside. There were about thirty in total.

'Ultra-Reality consoles,' Adam breathed. 'Must be what they mean by "games".'

'There aren't any screens,' Harm observed, crossing to another fire door on the other side of the room. 'How can you see what you're playing?'

'The screen's in your head,' Adam told her. 'You see what the characters would see and your thoughts control their every movement.' *But what games have Geneflow been using Dad's system and my brainwaves to develop?* He opened a drawer below one of the desktops and pulled out a scrunched-up bundle of wires and electrodes. 'Ultra-Reality uses Think-Send tech. There are no controllers.'

'Think-to-click,' Loner hissed behind them.

Adam felt cold quiver through his bones. 'Yes.' He

looked over at the raptor, suddenly intimidated by his size and presence. 'That was one of Dad's pet phrases for selling U-R. How could you know it?'

Loner stared at the consoles, shifting his weight from one foot to another. 'I read it in a file.'

Harm had been peering back through the door. 'If that map was right, this corridor should lead to the cave system – passing the main lab on the way.' She sighed. 'I can't wait to get out of here.' She turned back to the room.

Adam was about to agree when someone ran up behind them. He swung round, heart jumping into his throat – but it was only Chen. 'Uh, Loner . . . Did you get Doc Marrs's email address out of one of those files? I need to double-check I got the right one.'

'I . . . I will try to find it again.' Nodding, Loner followed him from the room.

Harm looked at Adam. She still had pasta sauce on her face. 'Can I help you here?'

'Not really,' Adam admitted.

She shrugged. 'Then I guess I'll make out I'm useful by helping Loner look for that file.'

Alone in the quiet games room, Adam wondered which of the consoles would give him access to the sea-creature-control program. *If the system's on a network, maybe they all will*, he thought, and fired up the nearest U-R set. The green light flashed, then shone at him, unblinking. Heart beating faster, he plugged in the tangled wire to the sensor port and placed the special pressure pads on the backs of his hands and just below each ankle with the speed and skill of an old pro – because with this system, that was exactly what he was. He'd been the test-subject for all the early versions of Think-Send, and a lot of the Ultra-Reality hardware *and* software had been built exclusively for Adam to test. *That was me*, he thought, *the cheapest guinea pig in town – playing the coolest demos in the world.*

As soon as he closed his eyes, he felt the familiar digital darkness swamp his senses as a new set of rules for reality asserted themselves in his brain. He felt the start-up system literally jolt through him, testing the Think-Send connections – a tap on the hand and a tickle on the feet – and then with no further ceremony he was into the console's world.

And there was no menu.

The title of the game that came screaming through his head in huge, blood-red letters was: *ALTA-VITA – A LIFE EXTREME.*

A familiar excitement raced through Adam as he found himself invited to select a dinosaur – just as he might have been asked to choose a car in a racing game. Some quite impressive graphics depicted the choices available: *Z-Utahraptor* or *Z-Velociraptor.*

After his experiences on Raptor Island, the feel of the dinosaurs in his head was almost too intense. He felt lost in his own body, cut-off, and all he could feel was the presence of the raptors waiting to be chosen. The Brute offered more power. The Velociraptor promised higher intelligence.

Adam decided on the Vel option. *Think to click*.

'Sure?' asked a soft, synthetic voice in his head.

Another firm yes — and Adam gasped as a bolt of electricity seemed to smash through him. He was suddenly taller, looking down on a vivid jungle. His vision wasn't quite right; he couldn't focus in the usual way.

'You now have both binocular and monocular vision,' the synthetic voice advised. 'Experiment with focusing with only one eye at a time. Note you will find a blind spot in your vision of approximately twenty degrees unless you turn your head behind you . . .'

Queasily he tried to focus on a nearby tree. He soon could see well enough to know only one type of leaf had been rendered and duplicated, but a thought like that was hard to hold onto — there was so much else to take his attention. Adam almost stumbled; his body shook as he did so, as though he weighed a ton. And there was something pulling and dragging at his lower back from behind. *A tail*, he thought, *I have a tail*.

Oh, God. It's like I'm . . .

Like I'm Loner.

It was getting too much. *Quit. Now.* Adam thought to exit the application. Nothing happened. He was trapped in the body of a virtual Velociraptor, and now someone was striding into view. An ordinary man in an ordinary grey suit. Adam felt a twinge of hatred.

'Target sighted,' the voice said.

Get me out of this. Adam closed his raptor eyes. *Quit!*

The jungle was blacked out, but he could hear the man screaming in terror, could feel a surge of fury twisting his emotions and his Z. raptor body stumbling forward almost on instinct.

Quit!

But his tail was helping him balance and his steps were getting faster . . .

'Kill the enemy,' said the voice, with relish. 'Kill with freedom. This is the *Alta-Vita*. Kill him.'

QUIT! QUIT!

And suddenly Adam was falling through space, landing with a thump back in his own body again. He panted for breath, an awful nausea buzzing in his stomach. U–R had always been way more than just a game – everything in it was heightened. But *that* simulation . . .

It's like the game controls you.

He shuddered to feel the shadow of his dinosaur self, still lurching about in his brain's backwaters. A high-scores table had started rolling over the virtual blackness, and Adam tried to focus on the list of names and numbers to bring himself back down from his dislocation and leave him better prepared to try again to find the sea monster program.

4,788,025 . . . . LOWE, N.

2,490,725 . . . . MOORE, J.

2,346,975 . . . . VETRI, V.

An ear-splitting alarm tore violently through the Games Room, like a Brute's roar in Adam's ears. He sat bolt upright, yanked away the headset, sweat prickling through every pore. As he peeled off the pressure pads he realized he could smell burning. The console? No . . .

The smoke was seeping in from outside.

The next moment Loner smashed through the door, soaking wet. Adam jumped up in alarm. Sprinklers in the ceiling were filling the smoky corridor with fierce showers of water but the acrid stink of burning plastic still carried from—

'The records room?' Adam stared at Loner in confusion, still tugging his mind from the last grips of Ultra-Reality. *Which raptor will you choose?* 'What . . . what happened?'

'Don't know,' Loner barked over the alarm. 'Chen sent the mail, Harm tried to load a disk and . . .'

'A fire started?' Adam jerked properly awake and staggered across the room. 'Are they all right? We've got to get them. This alarm, it'll bring everyone in the building running.'

'Wait.' Loner flicked out his tail, curled it around Adam's arm. 'Chen called his ship. Did you stand down the defences?'

'I . . . I haven't found the interface yet,' Adam told him. 'Come on, first we've got to get Harm and Chen out of—'

A torrent of crackling blue energy smashed into Loner from the doorway, held him helpless in its bone-rattling grip. Adam was jolted clear of the raptor, smashing into a desk. He stared helplessly as a guard pushed into sight with an electro-shock gun; as Loner shook like a doll in the grip of an angry toddler, panting with pain as he curled into a ball.

'No!' yelled Adam. But his vision was blurring. Blackness was slipping into his pounding skull. As he blacked out completely he was glad he couldn't see Loner's death throes any longer.

20: Being Human

Adam woke with a splitting headache. It was cold. A rushing hum of power pulled at his ears – air conditioning or hard drives whirring, he wasn't sure. Memories tumbled through his mind like hot coals, and he barely dared open his eyes. It was like being trapped in a nightmare, when you know the horror of what you will find before your eyes meet it.

When he did look he caught movement just metres away – a Brute striding towards him. He flinched – then realized the beast was only an image on a massive TV screen set into the wall opposite. Six smaller screens were ranged above it, but they were turned off. The main image was shaking as if the camera was swinging about, but with a start Adam recognized raptor eggs at the Brute's feet, lying in piles of sand and dirt.

Looking away, Adam took in his own surroundings. He was in a large rectangular room, painted white and painfully over-lit. As he recoiled from the glare, he found he was sitting on the floor, leaning up against a wall with his arms tied behind his back.

Straight ahead of him lay Loner, curled up on a huge steel slab. From the circular lamps arranged above it, Adam guessed it was an oversized operating table. The raptor was just barely breathing. A guard in a hazard suit, cradling his shock gun, watched as a woman and J.J.'s friend, Dr Haskins – all dressed like surgeons in scrubs and plastic aprons – hooked Loner up to a half-dozen high-tech monitors. With a stab of fear, Adam saw trays full of medical instruments had been ranged around the beast's body.

Must be the labs on Level Two, he thought helplessly. *This is so not good.*

'I hadn't expected to see you again, Adam. From your physical condition, I assume you washed in on the wreck of the *Hula Queen*?' A short, neat, petite woman stepped in front of him, her skin just a shade lighter than Harm's. A sad little smile creased her unblemished face. 'You were touching the raptor when my guard shocked him, so I'm afraid you received a little of his punishment.'

'Samantha Josephs,' croaked Adam. He watched her as warily as he would a Brute. 'Where's Harmony, and Chen?'

She nodded beside him. Adam saw Chen and

Harm were trussed up just as he was. Chen was beginning to stir.

'Your father's not with you,' Josephs surmised. 'I wonder who you've turned to for support in his absence – Agent Chen, or the too-clever raptor here?' She shook her head. 'Neither choice is a good one.'

'Josephs?' Chen's voice sounded like his throat had been sanded down. 'Glad . . . I found you.'

The woman turned to him primly. 'I can only assume you're here because someone has learned about the money I paid you to stop your investigation into Geneflow's affairs. Had I known then what an incompetent you obviously are, I would have paid you a good deal less.'

'I got past your guards and all the way down here without your knowing a thing about it,' Chen said smugly. 'Though I guess you've been kind of busy this morning after we stirred up the wildlife, huh?' He looked at the guard. 'Was it you who took the lift up top to see why your buddies hadn't come back? If you'd only taken the stairs you might have run straight into us.'

The guard said nothing but gripped his gun a little tighter.

'Don't let our prisoner rile you, Ford,' Josephs told him coolly, then turned her attention back to Chen. 'What is it you want, I wonder. More money to keep your mouth shut? I'm afraid our plans have come on a little too far for that to seem attractive . . .'

'I want answers,' Chen said. 'I want to know what you've been doing.'

'Then perhaps you shouldn't have set fire to my research centre.' The look in Josephs' brown eyes had hardened. 'If my team hadn't already scanned and archived the data . . .'

'I don't know how that fire started. But you know, you seem kind of angry, Sammy,' Chen needled her. 'Did we spoil your morning, setting off your dinosaurs like that, huh?'

'Promising specimens have been destroyed.' Haskins spoke like a doctor giving bad news. 'Not one of the *Velociraptor* eggs survived.'

So even the one he took away was bad. 'I'm crying the world's smallest tear,' Adam murmured, not quite brave enough to say it loud and proud.

'Now our hopes lie with the Brutes' eggs.' Josephs turned to a big TV screen. 'Or perhaps with this *Velociraptor* you've adopted.'

'Loner?' Adam said automatically. 'What are you doing to him?'

Josephs grinned. 'Is that what you call him? Loner?'

'It's what he calls himself. He knows he's different from the other raptors.' He couldn't resist the chance to goad her. 'It's Loner who's really messed up your experiment – maybe with a little help from my brainwaves in the Think-Send you've been using. Your own creation turned against you.'

He wanted to see Josephs dismayed or angry, but she simply looked at Haskins. 'I honestly thought this Vel was another failure, at first. But if he really remembers his past . . .'

'It could mean a breakthrough far ahead of schedule,' Haskins agreed.

'Remembers what past?' Adam asked.

'Never mind Loner.' Chen nodded to the unconscious Harm. 'I want to know why you've abducted this kid, and Lisa Brannigan and all the others. Why you took Death Row cons from across the United States – and what you did to them.' He strained forward angrily. 'I want to know what *I* did by letting you go, what I helped you put together here.'

'So you can pull it back down again, single-handed?' Josephs seemed amused. 'I've brought you here to give *me* answers. You must tell me more about "Loner", as you call him. I want to know exactly how he has helped you. I want you to describe his behaviour and his abilities.'

'What about your spy-cams in the raptors?' Adam asked. 'Haven't you seen for yourselves?'

She waved to the large screen. 'We've been monitoring the different packs through camera implants in the alpha males and females. "Loner" here fell sick and was shunned by his pack, and so has escaped scrutiny.'

'Lucky him,' Chen muttered. 'We're not helping you, Sammy.'

'Not even if I agree to help you?' Josephs asked. 'I'm a scientist, not a murderer. Cooperate and I'll turn you loose once the experiment is over. Leave you on this island.'

Chen sneered. 'And that's not a death sentence?'

'A true death sentence is handed out with good reason,' said Josephs. 'That was certainly true in the case of Neil Richard Lowe.'

Adam was lost. 'Who?'

'He's a killer who preyed on those weaker than himself,' Josephs replied. 'All our convicts had a strong predator's instinct, of course, that was the whole point. But some took to the raptor simulations better than others. And some, like Mr Lowe, were clearly in a league of their own.'

'I played that simulation,' said Adam. 'Why make people pretend to be raptors?'

Josephs looked at him. 'For the day when they would *become* raptors.'

Adam felt suddenly colder than the air-con could ever make him. 'Neil Richard Lowe . . .' He pictured the high-score table he'd seen in the simulator, one of the names shining in his memory: *LOWE, N.*

Without even thinking his mind pushed the word and letters together into a pattern.

Lowe-N. And an R for Richard.

Loner.

'Oh, no.' Adam fought against the tears of helplessness he could feel bunching in his throat. 'No, no, no . . .'

'Get out of here,' Chen said hoarsely. 'I'm not buying that. We saw the bone pit. We saw the remains of those cons.'

'You saw the remains of their bodies,' Josephs informed him casually. 'Their minds had already been uploaded to our computer model, adapted for our purposes, and then downloaded into the original raptor embryos.'

'That . . . That's why you stole the brain-map research from Mindcorp?' Adam felt sick. He remembered the deformed, hunchbacked Brute shouting at Loner in the jungle – it hadn't been ordering him to kneel low. It was shouting 'Neil Lowe'. Somehow it had made the connection. And when it had picked on Harm – 'Sweet Harmony, Perfect Harmony' – and said 'you're mine . . .'

It really did know her, he realized. *That thing was all that was left of Harm's father. And it died trying to protect her.*

Adam was glad Harm was asleep right now.

Chen looked sickened. 'You tricked all those con-victs into coming here, did *that* to them – and then fed them to the things they'd become?'

'If we'd left them on Death Row they would have been killed uselessly,' Josephs reminded him. 'At least this way their deaths helped science.'

'Bull! This isn't science. It's plain sick.'

'We're working to build a new society, Agent Chen,' Josephs argued, 'free from murder, free from crime.'

'Only because you're choosing what they think,' Chen shot back, 'as well as how they look.'

'The sick raptors . . .' Adam stared at Josephs. 'Are they the ones who remembered something of who they used to be?'

'Yes.' She crossed to check the connections between Loner and the machines. 'In most cases it drove them mad. Although Lowe was a psychopath even before his conversion. A master manipulator. One of the most dangerous men we had here.'

'But . . .' Chen looked way out of his depth. 'Why would anyone want to take a human mind and put it in the body of a raptor?'

Josephs didn't look up from her work. 'Because ultimately it's easier to change ourselves than to change our world.'

Chen swore. 'You want to change people into *dinosaurs*?'

'Don't be an imbecile,' said Josephs. 'This is

simply the first step on a long journey of evolution.' She crossed to the still-sleeping Harm and nudged her with the toe of her boot, exposing the gash on the back of the girl's head. 'See how fragile people are. You must know better than anyone, John, you've seen so much death in your time . . . So many people killed every day. So many people who still had so much to give.' She crossed back to the slab on which Loner lay. 'Imagine if we could heal ourselves fully after trauma, the way a reptile or amphibian can. A lizard can re-grow its tail, a sala- mander can regenerate whole limbs or even parts of its spine.' She smiled. 'Like the Z. rex, our Z. raptors contain molecule machines that can rebuild dam- aged cells — but we have made the healing process more powerful still by incorporating amphibian DNA into their genetic makeup.'

Chen sneered. 'Taken from those things in the sea that wrecked my ship?'

'The guardians are the result of some of our less successful experiments in DNA sampling,' Josephs conceded. 'But put to excellent use here as attack animals.' She looked between Adam and Chen. 'You still don't grasp it, do you? Did it ever occur to you to look up what "gene flow" even means? It's the transfer of genetic material from one population to another; amphibians into reptiles—'

'And humans into dinosaurs,' Adam whispered.

'The dinosaurs thrived on Earth for hundreds of millions of years,' said Josephs. 'We *Homo sapiens* face extinction after a few hundred thousand. Pollution, climate change, weapons of mass destruction – sooner or later we must destroy either the planet or ourselves.'

One of the female doctors, an Asian woman with scraped-back hair, joined in the speech making. 'Global agreement to cut back on carbon emissions or reduce the stockpile of nuclear weapons can only delay the inevitable,' she insisted, like she was quoting some mad scientist handbook. 'Humanity needs to adapt.' She looked at Josephs. 'It needs strength and boldness of vision.'

Josephs smiled approvingly. 'Now science has shown us that our bodies are simply vehicles for our genes, as a race we must take control of them and achieve our true potential or suffer the consequences of our inaction.'

Adam shook his head. 'How is making two kinds of dinosaur fight each other to the death going to achieve anything?'

'You're missing the point entirely.' Josephs switched on a monitor set into a console beside Loner and it began to fill with data. 'Our original aim with the Z. rex project was to create a highly trained, obedient slave-animal. When that beast developed free thought, however primitive, it suggested more exciting possibilities.'

'Oh, I bet you just peed yourselves with excitement,' drawled Chen.

'Our ultimate aim is to combine the human and dinosaur forms into a hybrid creature,' said Josephs, ignoring him. 'The raptors are among the most intelligent dinosaurs, but it's still not possible to upload a human personality into the brain of an animal and expect it to remain stable. We will have to manipulate many generations of raptor to achieve the proper balance. Evolution is a multi-layered story.'

Haskins nodded with enthusiasm. 'Starting with the marriage of human ambition and bestial instinct.'

Adam felt he was starting to understand. 'You took the minds from human predators 'cause they were closest to *animal* predators.'

'It was my job to assess the prisoners,' Haskins revealed. 'They were split according to their I.Q. score and how they performed on the Ultra-Reality simulation.'

'The smartest ones were made into Vels,' said Adam.

'Both raptor breeds were programmed with the instinct to preserve human life to feed to their young at the first hatching.' Josephs gestured to Harm. 'By keeping people like her prisoner – people we brought to the island – they would have the opportunity to study human behaviour over a

period of months, awakening unconscious connections within their minds . . . reminding them of their
own human inheritance.'

Chen shook his head in disgust. 'All these men and
women fighting so hard to stay alive . . . dragged
here just to help along your sick experiment.'

Haskins ignored him. 'The Brutes had more of
their humanity repressed than the Vels,' he said.
'You've seen the difference, I'm sure. The Brutes
would occasionally kill humans despite their conditioning. They've behaved like typical animals in the
wild. But the Vels cooperated as a tribe, learned to
use human tools and weapons . . . even went so far
as to move their camp from the wilds outside the
military base into the base itself, fully at home in a
human dwelling place.'

Josephs glanced at the screen, which still showed
a blurred view of Brute eggs. 'Unfortunately, with
their human traits closer to the surface, the Vels have
proved more prone to mental breakdown.'

Chen nodded. 'Lucky for your "studies" that your
hidden door backed onto their sick room, huh? If
they'd been playing all-night card games in there
you might've found the coming and going harder.'

'We had hoped the Vels' offspring would prove
more stable,' said Haskins. 'But now we'll never know.'

'We can look to enhance and strengthen the
human genes in the Brute hatchlings,' Josephs

consoled him. 'What we learn from dissecting the mind of "Loner" could offer several short cuts through the process.' She held up a sinister-looking surgical tool. 'He's survived the mental imbalance, and seems to have come through with plenty of human traits intact . . .'

'Just say you crack this crazy process of yours,' Chen said. 'D'you really think anyone's gonna thank you for sticking their brain into one of these dinosaur things?'

'When this technique is perfected, the finest scientific minds need never die,' Josephs proclaimed. 'The bodies that house them will be close to indestructible – and should the worst happen, can easily be uploaded again to a *new* form.'

'This is all wrong!' Adam shouted.

'It is simply radical and different, so you fear it instinctively. I suppose you feel that no one should have such power.' Her sympathetic smile hardened to a sneer. 'Well they do, now. And they will use it.'

'But you don't have to cut Loner open,' Adam protested. 'Just talk to him.'

'His cells will talk to me, clearly and honestly.' Josephs looked at Loner's body on the slab. 'Lowe laid here while we took his mind . . . now here he is again as we take his life.' She turned to the guard. 'Ford, we've wasted enough time on enlightening our guests. Take the children to my office.' She turned to the Asian woman. 'Doctor Lee, once you've finished setting up here, start recording their impressions of "Loner"'s behaviour. If they give you any trouble . . .'

Dr Lee looked unhappily down at the floor, but nodded.

'As for Agent Chen . . .' Josephs shook her head. 'Too dangerous. I think we'd best take you through the hidden door upstairs and let the Brutes find you. Give them one more for their feast.'

'You just can't let those monsters kill so many innocent people!' Chen shouted. The guard, Ford, hauled him roughly to his feet – but as he did so, Chen butted him in the stomach, shoving him back against Loner on the slab. Haskins ran forward to help restrain Chen, but the agent planted a boot in his stomach and sent him tumbling into a tray of instruments that clattered all over the tiled floor. Ford, staggering back from the slab, blasted Chen with the shock gun. With a high-pitched yell, Chen collapsed to the floor.

Josephs stared at him, flustered and seething with anger. 'Deal with him first, Ford. Do it.'

Ford nodded, and Adam stared helplessly as the guard hauled Chen's body out of the room and the door swung shut behind them.

'Now.' Josephs glared down at Adam. 'I trust you and the girl will prove a little more cooperative?'

'Sam, wait.' Dr Lee sounded concerned as she pointed to the screen. 'What's this?'

Through the camera implanted in the male Alpha-Brute minding the makeshift hatchery, Adam recognized One-Eye and the rangy female, the two Brutes who'd attacked Loner back by the bone pit. They bobbed their heads low, turned down their claws, acting passive. Then, without warning, they started trampling the eggs, cracking them open, stooping to devour the fleshy innards. The Alpha-Brute rushed to the attack, spitting acid at One-Eye and slashing the smaller one with his claws.

Haskins, still on his knees, was watching in horror. 'What're they doing?'

'Those are the last of the eggs.' Josephs had bunched her fists. 'If they're destroyed we'll have no hatchlings for study at all!' She yanked a two-way radio from her lab coat. 'Ford, come in. Come *back*.' She shook it crossly. 'Damned batteries . . . Ford, this is Josephs; forget Chen, you've got to . . .' As the carnage on screen continued, she gave up on the radio and ran to the door, hurling it open and pursuing the guard down the corridor. 'Ford! Ford, get back here . . .'

But Adam saw that One-Eye had something clamped in his clawed hand. Something small and metal. One-Eye rammed it into the Alpha-Brute's jaws. The point of view blurred as the beast staggered backwards – and then the screen flared red before sputtering into static.

Haskins seemed shell-shocked. 'Was that a *grenade* shoved into its mouth?'

Dr Lee nodded. 'Must've been taken from the armoury. Explosion took out the cameras . . .'

'My cue to take out *you*.'

Adam started at the sound, the now familiar unearthly whisper, and again as Loner jerked upright on the slab. His terrible injuries seemed all but healed. He looked stronger, more fearsome than ever.

Haskins flinched. 'What the—?'

He'd barely said a word before the raptor swung his arm in a lethal arc, slicing open the man's chest. Haskins fell soundlessly, eyes wide, a huge red patch spreading over his torso.

'You can't be awake!' Dr Lee backed away. 'I gave you enough sedative to keep down an animal twice your size . . .'

She grabbed one of the surgical tools. But as she lunged forward to use it, Loner kicked her into the blank screen on the wall so hard that glass and skull split open together. She slid down the wall, leaving a bloody trail on the whitewashed bricks.

Just then Josephs re-entered. There was no sign of Ford.

Loner loomed over Josephs.

'Don't kill her, Loner!' Adam shouted. 'We need to know what else Geneflow are planning, where their other bases are.' He shut his eyes as he heard bones crack as Loner attacked. 'Don't!'

Then Josephs gave a low, agonized wail that chilled Adam's blood.

Opening his eyes he saw a scarlet pool spreading from beneath her back. Recoiling, Adam rolled over, nudging up beside the unconscious Harm.

Loner took a step backwards, as if shocked by what he'd done. Or maybe shocked only by how easy and how swift his revenge had been.

Adam looked over at the raptor. 'I know they hurt you,' he whispered, 'but . . . you didn't have to . . .'

'It's all right.' Josephs turned her head, staring wide-eyed at Adam, her voice and breathing steady. 'I'm still alive. It'll be like the last three months never happened, that's all.'

She's in shock, thought Adam, fear and revulsion clouding numbly inside him. *Losing it.*

'The work will go on, you'll see.' A trickle of blood leaked from her mouth as her eyes slowly closed. 'All you've put yourself through . . . and you haven't even won breathing space.'

Then her head lolled back. Josephs was dead.

Loner just stood there. Grinning in a room of corpses.

'You killed them all?' Adam whispered.

'I guess that's what I do,' said Loner softly. 'Impossible little old me.' And he leaned over Adam. Still grinning.

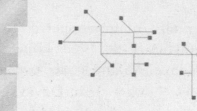

21: Me, Killer

Adam trembled as Loner reached behind him and cut his ropes with a flick of one claw. He rubbed his aching wrists. His mind was still reeling with all that had just happened, all he had learned. Since he'd washed up on the island he'd been thinking of the raptor as another Zed, a misunderstood monster acting basically for good. But now he knew Loner's true heritage.

And alone with him Adam was terrified.

'It's over now.' Loner lifted him gently onto the slab. 'What is wrong?'

'Nothing,' Adam whispered. *Just what did you do before you became this?*

'Where is Chen?' Loner asked. 'Is Chen all right?'

'No. He was unconscious like Harm.' Adam wrung his hands miserably. 'A guard took him up above to be given to the Brutes for the feast.'

'With the eggs destroyed there will be no feast. The prisoners are safe.' Loner glanced around. 'The guard didn't come back?'

'Not yet.'

'And Harm is still asleep?'

'She hasn't woken since the fire.' He looked into Loner's lantern eyes. 'Look – Lisa, David, Doctor Stone and the others . . . surely we need to—'

'I told you, they're not in danger any more.' Loner kept his gaze fixed on Adam. 'My followers have smashed the eggs and killed the other Brutes. They won't harm the captive humans.'

'Followers? You mean the one-eyed Brute and his girlfriend . . . they, like, serve you?' Adam frowned. 'But they attacked you yesterday. Half-killed you.'

'And I beat them,' Loner bragged. 'That proved my power to them, made them willing to follow me. Especially once I'd killed their queen . . .'

'But why would they kill their own kind just 'cause you told them to?' Adam didn't get it. 'You're a Vel, the enemy—'

'I was an outsider, just as they were,' Loner insisted. 'You saw their pathetic gang – bottom of the pecking order, always fed last and passed over for breeding. I encouraged them to take revenge on those that spurned them – just as I did.'

Adam swallowed dryness in his throat. 'So . . . now what?'

'They planned to have hatchlings of their own, which will feed on the humans . . .' The raptor barked his laughter. 'But now they've done what was required, I will kill them – before they kill me. Lisa and David will be so happy, won't they? They'll be pleased with me. All the humans will. Everything has gone to plan.'

Adam's unease was growing. Loner sounded wilder, rougher. 'Uh . . . *your* plan?'

'Did Josephs say things to you about me?' Loner asked suddenly. 'About who I used to be?' Loner stared down at him, his scaly lips twitching. 'Bad things?'

'N . . . no.' Adam couldn't keep the tremble from his voice. Sitting on this cold slab, surrounded by bodies, alone with . . . what?

A psychopath, Josephs had said. *A manipulator. One of the most dangerous men here.*

'She did, didn't she?' Loner tipped his head to one side. 'You know about me now. Don't you.'

'I . . . I know you've been through things I could never imagine,' Adam began. 'I mean, it's no wonder you wanted to help the people here. Deep down you must've known that *you* were human once.' He hesitated, looking into Loner's eyes. 'And I know that whoever you were before this happened and whatever you did, you're different now. You . . . you've changed.'

'Changed.' Loner seemed to taste the word in his mouth, jaws twitching. Then he sighed, a gust of hot, wet breath. 'Oh, Adam. I haven't changed at all . . .'

Suddenly the raptor pounced forward, claws splayed, jaws cranking open. Adam shouted out in horror as Loner grabbed hold of him by the shoulders and slammed him back against the slab.

'What are you doing?' Adam struggled helplessly. 'Let me go.'

'You kids, you're so trusting, aren't you? So stupid. I told you, stupid is good. People like me, we *love* stupid.' Loner's jaws swung shut, the scaly muzzle grazing Adam's cheek. 'Oh, but I'm forgetting – there *are* no people like me. Not now.'

'Josephs said it was impossible to put a human mind inside an animal,' Adam whimpered, as if parroting the words might make them true.

'Then we know better than she does,' Loner hissed. 'Because I know exactly who I used to be . . . and all that I can become.'

'But you . . . you helped us.' Adam couldn't accept what was happening. 'Harm and Lisa and David and me – you risked your life for us over and over.'

'Course I did. That was the plan, I *had* to keep you alive.' Loner bared his teeth in a crocodile grin, his voice harder, rougher. 'I always knew that when this was over I'd need witnesses. Grateful survivors who'd testify to my goodness, my kindness . . .' A quiet chittering sound rose from his throat like a snake's rattle – or like laughter. 'That's why I can't leave any incriminating evidence behind. Like Josephs and her scientists. Like those files.'

'*You* . . . set the fire in the data room?'

Loner glared down at him. 'Chen and Harm will believe it was an electrical fault. They'll think it was Josephs' men who hit them from behind.'

Adam felt a rush of helpless anger. 'The stuff in there could've helped us to nail Geneflow. Whatever they're planning—'

'*WHO CARES?*' Loner snorted in Adam's face, his features alive with little jumps and tics. 'Geneflow gave me new life . . . *higher* life, just like they said they would when I was stuck on Death Row. They tried to trick me . . . but I tricked them. Tricked everyone!' He squeezed a little harder and Adam gasped as the claw tips pinched his skin. 'Without Harm and Agent Chen and the others to speak for me, when rescue came I'd be put to death or locked up. A dangerous animal. A killer.' He shook his head. 'Not again. Been there. Done that.'

Adam was trying not to whimper like an animal himself. 'You . . . you think that just 'cause you helped people, Doctor Marrs will let you run off into the wild?'

'Chen contacted his ship. Help is coming soon. And Chen will owe me for saving him and Stone. He won't like it but he'll agree to take me off this island . . . and once I'm on board I can make him take me anywhere.' Loner made the chittering noise again. 'Such a shame you had to find out the truth about me. You'd have helped to convince him, I know.'

Chen knows the low-down on you too, thought Adam. *But the moment he mentions it, Loner will have to kill him – along with anyone else he's told . . .*

'Please don't hurt me,' Adam begged. 'I won't say anything, I promise.'

'Of course you will, Adam. The first chance you get. Because you're desperate and you're scared.' Loner breathed in deeply, his jaws widening and stringing saliva. 'I never truly appreciated what fear is until I could smell it . . . taste it . . .' His claws clacked together menacingly. 'So many lives will be mine for the taking. The one, true Z. raptor. Think of the hearts I shall bite out and gorge on when I am truly free again.' His jaws twitched and trembled as he edged closer to Adam's chest.

'Wait!' In Adam's terror, inspiration struck. 'No one's going to defend you to anyone if you kill me. I haven't turned off the attackers in the sea, remember? No one can get to this island or away from it till I do.'

Loner's hideous grin didn't falter. '*I* can use Ultra-Reality.'

'Not any more you can't,' said Adam, speaking through gritted teeth. 'You saw that "games room", the headsets are designed for human heads, not yours.'

'Then Harm can use it. Or one of the others.'

'Do they look like gamers to you? They won't know how.' Adam gasped again as he felt trickles of blood run down his bare arms. 'If they mess up, the system will go into lockdown and then you'll never get away from here.' He looked into the raptor's eyes. 'You . . . you still need me.'

Slowly Loner pulled away his claws. Adam wiped at the slick, sticky blood on his arms, wincing as he did so, glaring at the raptor.

'All right. But no tricks. No stalling.' Loner pushed Adam off the slab, gripped him by the back of the neck and forced him across the room, past Josephs' body and Harm's beside it, out into the main passage.

Adam fought to keep his voice steady. 'What do I get once I've done this for you?'

Loner kicked open a door and shoved Adam down the stairs towards the base's bottom level. 'I'll spare your father on board Chen's boat.'

Like I can believe anything you say, Adam thought bitterly, shivering in the concrete cool.

'Perhaps I'll even let you run.' Loner went on. 'But I wouldn't try running up these stairs to your friends above.' He smashed open the door to Level Three and pushed Adam through. 'The last of my pet Brutes will be on their way to join me now their work is done. I told them where to find the hidden keypad and carved the entry code on the wall of the sick room.'

That's why he had looked so shifty and kept his back to the wall as the rest of us ran through, Adam realized. *Hiding what he'd done.*

'They should be here any time now.' Loner kept pushing him onward. 'The three of us can take care of Geneflow's last guard . . . then once Harm is awake to see it, I'll kill the Brutes too.' He clicked his claws as they passed the ash-black, twisted ruin of the records annexe. 'Thanks to me, the ordeal of these poor stranded castaways will be over at last. Shame you won't be around to celebrate with them.'

Finally Loner pushed him into the A–V Unit. Adam tried not to stare at the heavy door on the other side of the room, which Harm had said led on to the cave tunnels – and ultimately freedom. *The way out to the Brute's camp must be a kilometre or so from here,* he thought grimly. *You'd be dead before you got a grip on the door handle.*

'Spent a lot of happy hours in this room.' Loner was gazing round. 'The sense of power that raptor sim gave us . . . The realism. The hunting. It was addictive. So addictive.'

Adam barely heard him, feeling numb as he sur-

veyed the terminals. If he stood down Raptor
Island's defences, Loner would escape and could kill
countless people. If he faked his obedience, then
Chen's other ship would cruise straight into the sea
monsters; Adam might be killing his own dad.

How could he decide what to do?

'Well?' Loner made a threatening noise in the
back of his throat. 'I warned you. No stalling.'

'I'm not sure . . . wait.' Adam realized the console
and tabletop in the far corner had marks and trails
in the dust – signs it had been used. 'It could be this
one.'

Loner forced him down into the chair. 'Get on
with it.'

Adam fought to stay calm, knowing he'd need
all his concentration to go straight into using
Think-Send in a completely foreign program. The
Z. raptor simulation had been bad enough, but to
actually control those sea monsters . . .

He started up the console, hooked himself into
the pads, picked up the headset and hesitated, afraid
of what he might find inside the virtual world.
Afraid of choosing wrongly. Afraid of Loner's claws
slicing into him the moment he was through.

'Do it,' Loner grunted.

Slowly, carefully, Adam put on the headset. As he
closed his eyes, a sensation of pressure formed in his
ears and temples. A soft turquoise glow appeared in

his mind, resolving itself into a kind of electronic grid. *Yes*, he thought. *This is the interface.*

There was a strip of yellow at the bottom – a shore, presumably – and then different shades of blue, each relating to a zone of either depth or distance. No fancy menus or start-up screens – this program was simply a tool of control.

Adam saw a large red boat-shaped graphic flashing in one of the grid squares. The *Pahalu*, out at sea, waiting to sail to Raptor Island. And there, ranged all around the island's perimeter in a thin belt, were forty smaller, darker shapes.

The guardians. Primed and ready to attack.

Adam thought back to that night of terror when the *Hula Queen* sank, pictured J.J. or somebody sitting here, calmly moving and motivating the creatures around this virtual board, uncaring of the carnage they were creating and the life-or-death frenzy that followed.

It mustn't happen again, thought Adam. *But if I stop it, and Loner gets free . . .*

Dad could die either way.

Adam could almost feel the raptor's shadow hanging over him.

There were no instructions or prompts on this 'level' of the control game, but he didn't need them. It wasn't just convenience or favouritism that had caused Bill Adlar and his team to build Ultra-

Reality around Adam's mind – '*We're all agreed. You're one of the most instinctive gamers we've tested.*'

Adam braced himself. *Here's where I have to prove it.*

He let go of his thoughts, allowed the blue wash of the screen to stream deep into his mind, as though he was out there beneath the waves. In a sense, he supposed he was – the A-V Unit was in that part of the base built below sea level, closest to the tidal power station that fed the systems of this hidden outpost. That made it easier in Adam's mind to drift away through the concrete walls, through the winding caves and into the depths. He saw the black, ominous figures lying dormant in the water, waiting. Soon he could feel a kind of tension in his head, a tentative link with the sea creatures. Pressure rose in his ears, a sensation that he was really underwater, but still breathing. Still OK. He began to feel the monsters' liquid movements in the deep, still waters. The sound of distant engines carried to him, heavy and rumbling, weighing him down with their noisy shimmer. He could almost sense the intrusion of the sound in the monsters' minds. A trigger for their violence. He felt the tug of the rigid instructions that directed their behaviour. *Attack the ship – bite – disengage – turn – attack again . . .*

His mind began to cloud. Adam tried to drag his

focus away from the black shapes but by now his mind was hooked into their emptiness, the gaping dark of their consciousness held him fast. They were hungry for commands, for any contact, and he felt an overwhelming pity for these animals – butchered by Geneflow and turned into killing machines.

Keeping calm, ordering his thoughts, Adam forced himself to lift his senses out of the dark and concentrate again on the grid – to take control of the reef of creatures instead of drifting amongst them. This was the moment of decision. What would he do – switch off the creatures, or direct them to keep up their defence of the island waters? Or maybe . . .

Adam felt the dark seawater in his eyes like tears. He knew there was only one course of action he could take now.

I love you, Dad.

He concentrated on each dark spot in turn and fed through its final instructions . . .

22: Earth Shock

Adam was finishing up when he felt cold weight on his shoulder, a disembodied hand. Then a distant scream carried to him through the blurring dark-ness of the sea – *no, not the sea, I'm here in the A-V Unit, I'm not lost out there with the creatures, I'm back*—

'Adam!' It was his name being shouted, as if from a million miles away. With a jerk he realized it was Harm's voice.

'Harm, I'm here!' Adam shouted. 'The Games Room!' For a dizzying moment, he saw the real world overlaid on the grid – the green eye of the console, the lazy flourish of dust in the artificial light, Loner's claws . . .

Then the headset was in his hands. Wetness was brimming in his eyes, and he could hear Harm's footsteps racing closer.

Loner pressed his scaly snout up to Adam's face. 'One word of warning to her,' he snarled, 'and I'll kill her while you watch.'

Harm raced in, her arms still tied behind her

back. Loner left Adam and loped over, his head bobbing low in eager welcome. 'Thank God,' she panted, as the raptor sliced through the ropes round her wrists. 'Now can someone tell me what in the world's been happening while I was out? I wake up to find I'm lying in a blood bath and get out in time to find two Brutes coming this way. They've got one of Josephs' guards with them . . .'

'It is all right.' Loner put on his concerned act for her, and Adam glared at him hatefully. 'Those Brutes are on our side. They have turned on their pack with human weapons, saved your friends from the feast.'

Harm blinked, looking overwhelmed. 'They what?'

'And I've taken care of the sea monsters,' Adam told her, fighting to keep his voice steady. *I'm so sorry*, he told her silently. *If there had been any other way . . .*

'Do not be afraid, Harmony.' Loner stopped her crossing to Adam and gently pushed her in the other direction, motioning her to hide behind the desk. 'I shall protect you.'

Liar! Adam longed to yell the word, to warn Harm away. But that would get the two of them killed at once. His ragged nerves were chafed again by a dragging, splashing noise from the wet corridor outside. Moments later the thump of heavy footsteps signalled the arrival of the Brutes. One-Eye and the stooped, skinny female were carrying Ford's limp body between them; the guard was clearly dead. But what had happened to Chen?

Loner straightened to his full height, asserting himself as their superior. 'You have killed your pack brothers and sisters?'

One-Eye nodded, his eyes narrowed, his jaws darkened with blood. 'All of them.'

'And their eggs,' hissed his partner, an evil glint in her eyes.

'We brought you this.' One-Eye shook Ford's corpse. 'He had taken another soft-skin for the feast and was returning. He did not see us.'

'We hid,' the female added, casting nervous looks at her mate. 'We hurt him.'

'And these others.' One-Eye looked between Adam and Harm. 'They are also for us to kill?'

'No,' Loner snapped. '*They* are mine.'

One-Eye and the female bowed and bobbed their heads. They lowered Ford's body carefully to the floor and seemed to have some trouble withdrawing their claws from his corpse. Adam saw a metallic glint from something in Ford's shirt pocket; the same sheen he'd glimpsed on the TV in the lab when One-Eye disposed of the alpha-male in the makeshift hatchery . . .

Ford's stuffed with grenades. They've pulled the pins and turned him into a bomb to kill Loner—

'Harm, get down!' Adam shouted, throwing himself behind the desk and clamping his hands over his ears. At the same time, the Brutes turned and ran. Loner swung his head between the two groups—

Ford's body exploded in a storm of fire and noise that did its best to level everything in the room. Monitors shattered, desks and chairs splintered and burned, concrete was blasted from the walls and ceiling. Adam curled tightly in a ball. His back felt skinned raw, he smelled burning hair and choked on smoke and rock dust. Something fell on him.

Harm.

'You OK?' she said, her eyes wide and terrified. 'Am – am *I* OK, Adam?'

They got up together, leaning on each other for support. Adam looked her over briefly. 'You look OK. Does anything hurt?

'No,' she said. 'You?'

'I'm good.'

Squinting over her shoulder through the flames and smoke Adam saw a seven-foot silhouette stagger from the shattered room, screeching and spluttering with rage.

'He was going to betray the Brutes,' Adam murmured, 'but they betrayed him first.'

'He must be hurt.' Harm pulled away. 'We have to help him.'

'No, we don't,' Adam told her.

'But he got Josephs, he saved the others—'

Adam grabbed her hand. 'Trust me on this, Harm, Loner's been playing us all for fools. He's a born-again killer, only looking after us so we'd speak up for him when rescue finally came.'

'I don't believe it,' Harm began, as the scream of the female Brute, short and rattling, drilled through the smoke. 'He's always been—'

'There's no time to explain now!' Adam saw a thick crack in the wall beside them and cursed under his breath. 'We have to get out of here.' He dragged her towards the door that led to the caves. 'I don't know if we can make it through the caves before the whole thing falls apart, but . . .'

'What are you talking about?' Harm demanded.

'I used Think-Send to get through to the sea monsters,' Adam told her, ushering her through to the corridor that led on to the underground cave systems. 'There must be forty all together. Loner wanted me to shut them down. Instead I directed them here to destroy the tidal power plant – and the foundations of the base with it.'

She stared at him, disbelieving. 'You did what?'

'I didn't know what else I could do!' he shouted. 'Loner was going to kill me as soon as I was through, I couldn't let him leave the island on Chen's ship and do the same to everyone on board, could I?'

A massive tremor thundered through the building, almost knocking both of them to the rubble that once had been a floor.

'The whole place will flood!' Harm realized. 'The whole place could come crashing down on top of us.'

Adam nodded, trembling, as a long, choking bellow that sounded like One-Eye cut suddenly off. 'We can't get past Loner to reach the lift or the stairs. When he's finished with the Brutes, he'll outrun us, easy. Our only chance is to get to the beach through the cave network to the old Brute camp.'

'You saw the map, those passages stretch on forever—'

'A kilometre, maybe.'

'And God knows how many of them are below sea-level.' Harm closed her eyes. 'Please, tell me I never woke up. Tell me this is all a nightmare.'

The building shook again. 'It's a nightmare, all right.' Adam grabbed her wrist and pulled her away with him towards the caves. 'Now, *come on!*'

The two of them ran through the passage and found that plaster soon gave way to natural rock, the walls gradually widening into the gaping mouth of a cavern. Pale electric lanterns hung at regular intervals; they cast little light but left the encroaching shadows darker. Five electric scooters stood in a line – presumably for guards to travel to and from the Brute camp to study their subjects, just as they had crept in and out of the Vel camp upstairs. The ground shook again, knocking over two of the scooters. Adam picked up one and Harm grabbed another.

'How do they work?' Adam asked.

Harm shook her head. 'How should I know? Let's see.' She turned a black plastic key beside the handlebars and then stabbed at a button. Her bike hummed eerily into life. Adam did the same and twisted the throttle, the whine of the engine bleed-ing into a desolate howl from somewhere behind them.

'I'll tear you apart, kid!' he heard Loner scream. 'Her first, then you!'

Harm put a hand to her mouth as though she might be sick. 'He's killed the Brutes.' She acceler-ated jerkily away as another ear-splitting crack set the ground belly-dancing. The lanterns set into the walls flickered, and Adam was glad for the steady blue shine of his bike's headlamp as he headed after her. 'We've got a chance,' he told himself. 'Please, let us have a chance.'

The tunnel was winding, the ground cracked and

uneven, and the scooters gave a bone-jarring ride. Each time the ground shook, the vibrations struck a little harder and went on for longer. Adam almost lost his balance a dozen times, veering about clumsily, straining to see the turn of the tunnel in the blur of blue from the headlight. The run was reckless, but it had to be. He had no idea how fast a Z. raptor could sprint, but he could imagine how fast the seawater all around would flood the cave system he and Harm were speeding through. The thundering shudders were lasting longer, doing more and more damage.

It was Harm whose luck ran out first. The whole passage jumped as though kicked by a giant, and a large chunk of the roof fell and nearly crushed her. Swerving to avoid it, she lost control of the scooter, rode into the wall and fell heavily against the bare rock. Adam ditched his own scooter and ran to help her; in the blue blur of the headlight he saw her legs were raked with nasty gashes, and her cheek was scraped raw. Her scooter had fared even worse, with a twisted front wheel.

Adam cast a frantic look back down the tunnel. How far had they come? How close behind was Loner? 'You can ride with me,' he said. But as she tried to follow him over, she gasped and winced each time she put weight on her right leg. 'Is it broken?'

'I think I sprained my ankle,' she muttered.

A new noise carried to them as Adam lifted his scooter. Heavy footfalls on the rock, pounding like a steady heartbeat behind them.

Harm looked at Adam fearfully. 'Loner's coming.'

'Get on,' he told her, restarting the engine. As they pulled away, Adam barely managed to keep his balance as the ground grumbled again. Harm was holding on to his waist behind him, he could feel the shake in her skinny arms like a second engine. On the other side of the rumbling walls he could picture the dark shapes of the sea monsters massing in the deep, tearing into the base's foundations with the same remorseless power they had turned on the *Hula Queen*.

Then he heard a deep, creaking noise that seemed to thunder all around; the sound of solid stone straining under heavy duress, with a frothing, bubbling rumble building up beneath. Adam glimpsed boulders blocking the passage ahead, braked sharply to check the way forward.

'Oh, God,' Harm whispered.

Adam glanced behind – and through the thick gloom glimpsed a dark, tailed figure in the far distance racing towards them. Panic rising, he wheeled the bike forward a little way – far enough to see that the passage was impassable. 'Cave in,' he said helplessly. 'We'll have to climb over.'

He started up the pile, helping Harm manage with her bad ankle. The scraping beat of Loner's footsteps behind was quickening. And then the background creaking gave way to a wrenching, shattering boom, like a long-threatened storm had finally broken.

'It's hopeless,' Harm snapped, clinging to the rockpile. 'We can't outrun Loner!'

'And nothing can outrun *that*,' breathed Adam, staring over his shoulder as a wall of seething seawater came crashing into view, ready to dash them to pieces.

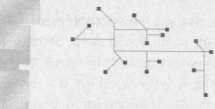

23: Slipping Away

As the foaming wedge of water swept towards them, Loner was snatched from sight. Adam turned desperately to Harm. 'We've got to get to the other side of this pile or we'll be crushed against it. We can do this!'

Harm looked into his eyes and nodded. He saw the tears there. And the resolve.

They scrambled like crabs over the rocks, braced themselves at the top, held their breaths – as the water struck them both like a freezing, frothing fist. In a moment it had thrown them fifty metres into the flickering darkness. Adam kicked wildly in a freezing soup of furniture and equipment – and found that it was kicking him back. Eyes stinging with salt, he looked around wildly for Harm in the boom and hiss of the rushing tide. As he did so, he nearly grazed his head on the rocky ceiling. The water level was rising with horrific speed. If the rushing torrent didn't drown him it would leave him crushed and grated raw. Surely if these tunnels led to the Brutes' beach they would rise above sea level soon and the water level would drop. *Surely . . .*

'Harm!' he yelled, swept helplessly along by the underground tsunami. 'Harm, where are you?' Files and chairs and a white-coated body plunged past him. Then something dark and reptilian bobbed towards him. He glimpsed a single bestial eye and jaws open wide.

With a scream of horror, Adam put up his hands in what he knew was a futile attempt to wrestle the thing away. But the jaws stayed slack. The eye was dark and dead.

The Brute's head had been severed from its neck; Adam found he was holding it like a float. Moaning with horror he pushed it away . . .

Just as Loner rose up in front of him with a hissing scream, jaws snapping, claws scything through the water to fillet him.

Adam lunged to his left, arms windmilling in a crawl, trying to escape — but debris slammed into his back and he went under, lost in icy subterranean blackness. Something closed on his leg. *Loner's jaws*, he thought with terror. But no, it was more wreckage of some kind, a chair maybe, dragging him down deeper. He kicked it free, but already his lungs were straining, his head was starting to spin. He glimpsed red stripes in the blackness, and the orange burn of an eye up close to his. He tried to push the raptor away, felt claws slice into his arm, cried out into the water, lost what little breath he had left. Black spots speckled his vision as that hideous reptile face pressed up close . . .

And then something big and heavy smashed Loner away from him. The dark rocky roof spun crazily above Adam as he broke through. In the still sputtering lantern-light he saw Loner clawing at a huge chunk of concrete that had him pinned against the wall. The raptor howled with pain, his barks and yowls hurling mad echoes around the tunnel as though some bigger, louder raptor was shrieking back at him.

Adam felt a moment's giddy triumph – but then the tip of Loner's tail twisted like a whip around his ankle and held him tight.

'No!' Adam yelled, trying to grasp hold of the rock wall and prevent his being pulled back underwater. 'Let go of me!'

The raptor said nothing, but his teeth were bared in a leering grin. Adam kicked and twisted round with the last of his failing strength but couldn't break Loner's grip. Water pushed down his throat. The darkness and the cold were slowing his movements, sapping his strength. Then Adam glimpsed something huge and dark sweeping through the water. For a split-second he thought it was one of the guardian creatures, breaking through into the tunnel. Then he saw the hard lines, the glinting edges.

It was the operating table from Josephs' lab. The scientist's slab where Neil Lowe had died and the thing he'd become had been born.

Glancing back over his shoulder, Adam realized that he was blocking Loner's view of the approaching danger. He flailed still more wildly, praying that his struggles would keep the raptor distracted.

'Kill you!' raged Loner, biting the air so close to Adam's neck, clawing at his concrete confinement. 'Kill you!'

'No!' Adam screamed back, transfixed by the operating table as it scythed through the seething seawater towards them. 'Kill *you!*'

At the last possible moment Adam stopped struggling and plunged down beneath the surface, using Loner's tail for leverage. One corner of the metal slab ploughed over his shoulder, missing him by millimetres. A fraction later it slammed into Loner's head with the force of a juggernaut, pulping the raptor's skull against the tunnel wall before resuming its headlong tumble through the water.

Stunned, Adam had barely a second to witness the gruesome aftermath before more rocketing debris caught the small of his back. Adam was smashed down underwater once more, scraping his arms and legs against the walls. He could barely process how many times he struck something hard or swallowed cold salt mouthfuls. The cave system was almost completely submerged. The last specks of consciousness began to drain from his mind as he seemed to spiral icily down . . . *down* . . .

Adam might have been out for seconds or maybe for minutes, but suddenly strong arms were lifting him, turning him onto his side. His ribs felt in pieces as he coughed up water, choking and retching for air, shivering cold on wet sand, his back and his head throbbing like crazy. As his eyes flickered open he found himself on a beach. A thick, wide stream of seawater was spewing from a cave in the cliffs, cutting through the shore and feeding back into the ocean.

'Easy, Adam.' Starting at the sound of David's voice, he turned feebly and saw the teacher's familiar weathered face lined with concern. 'You're OK. You washed out of there in one piece. Nothing broken.'

'Doesn't feel that way . . .' Adam tried to smile. 'I thought you were locked up . . .'

'We got out. Got all the other survivors out too.' David gave him a strained smile. 'Turns out our friendly neighbourhood guard J.J. had keys for all the rooms above ground as well as below – including the raptors' larder.'

'Though it took *me* to think of actually looking,'

came a familiar voice close by. Adam rolled over weakly to find Agent Chen kneeling close beside him. 'That a-hole Ford put me in with the other castaways – then ran into a pair of Brutes.'

'I know,' Adam muttered.

'So I checked out J.J., stole his keys, found the right one out of about a hundred and we all ran like hell – well, except for those who had to be carried.' Chen frowned at Adam. 'What's *your* story? What happened in there? That flood . . .'

'It was the sea monsters. They won't attack the *Pahalu* now. And Loner's dead. He tried to kill us . . .' Adam broke off in a coughing fit.

'Slow down,' Chen urged him.

'Loner never cared about anyone,' Adam muttered. 'He was just using us to get rescued.'

'He *what*?' David stared. 'You mean, after all these months—'

'Wait! Harm!' Adam shook his head, tried to lift himself up on his elbows. 'Where's Harm?'

'Uh . . . Lisa's waiting with the other survivors in the jungle,' David said, as if he hadn't heard.

Chen shared a look with him and nodded. 'See, Adam, when the earthquakes started, we high-tailed it down here to try and get you out through the beach tunnels. But I guess you beat us to it—'

'Where *is* she?' Adam realized David was blocking his way deliberately and struggled up. 'Harm!'

He saw her.

Lying on her back, her bloody legs bent at right angles to her body. Dr Stone was crouched over her, pinching her nose and breathing into her mouth.

'No!' Adam shouted, pushing past David to get to her. 'Harm, wake up, it's me!'

Stone didn't look up, putting his hands over her heart and starting compressions. 'Stay back, Adam. I know this is difficult for you, but . . .'

'You can't die, Harm,' Adam insisted, staring at her swollen face, her blue lips. 'I . . . I haven't even told you about your dad yet. He knew it was you – Perfect Harmony, Sweet Harmony.' He took her freezing cold hand in his own and held it tight. 'With all that Geneflow did to him, he still remembered. He still cared.' Tears were balling in his throat. 'He didn't die in Josephs' lab, all alone. He died protecting *you*.'

'John,' Stone called, 'the boy shouldn't have to see this.'

'We didn't tell him to wake up, Doc . . .'

'Harm, you can't die now,' Adam pleaded, shrugging off Chen's uncertain hands on his shoulders. 'We've made it, don't you see? We've—'

Suddenly Harm's back arched. She choked and puked water over herself. Adam shouted, and then laughed and pointed. 'You see that? She's back!'

'I hurt all over,' Harm said hoarsely.

'That just proves you're all right!' He whooped. 'She will be all right, won't she, Doctor Stone?'

'Aside from the headache you're giving her? I hope so.' Stone checked her eyes and her pulse. 'She needs rest. But I think she should pull through.'

'I'm glad you didn't get *your* friends killed, kid.' Chen was smiling, his hand held out to shake. Adam took it, and David put his own hand on theirs.

Stone rolled Harm onto her front, placed her head on one side. 'She needs fresh water and rest.'

'I'll find some coconut milk,' David offered.

'No way,' Harm gasped, her eyes still closed. 'David, there's, like, a ton of bottled water in the Geneflow storeroom.'

David looked at Chen. 'There is?'

'Through the sick-room door, down the steps, double doors on your left,' Chen confirmed. 'Start fattening up the survivors. Don't go crazy. Proper food's gonna be a shock to their systems — and I don't know how much toilet paper Josephs was hoarding . . .'

With a look hovering between amusement and disapproval, David turned and walked away.

Adam crouched beside Harm. 'It's going to be all right,' he whispered to her. 'It really is. The *Pahalu* can come in safely, get us out of here.'

'A good feeling, isn't it?' Stone smiled. 'Having hope again.'

Adam looked at him. 'Hope that we'll get back home?'

'Hope in being human,' Stone said quietly. 'For all their cleverness, Geneflow could only breed beasts that hate and kill and destroy. But for all our faults, people like us . . . we can mend. Mend and care and make better.' He shrugged. 'That's something I've forgotten these last washed-up years. I'm glad I've been given the chance to remember.'

Chen nodded. 'A new start, huh, Doc?'

'Why not?' Stone looked up at him. 'How much of our lives do we spend wishing we'd done things differently instead of making a difference now?'

'A Federal Agent doing time inside is sure going to be different,' said Chen.

Adam looked at him. 'You really think you'll go to jail?'

'I deserve to,' Chen accepted. 'And I will. But I need to swing a deal first. I'll serve out whatever sentence the judge decides – later. First, I've got to make somebody see we have to stop the rest of these Geneflow lunatics. With all I've witnessed here – with all I know now – I can't cool my heels in jail and trust some other jackass to take care of this. I'm seeing it through all the way.'

'There you go again, John.' Stone shook his head. 'A snap decision you'll be regretting for the rest of your life.'

'Next time I'll be going it alone, Doc,' Chen promised him. 'You've done enough for me, and I'll never be able to repay Pete and Brad and Doug and . . .' He trailed off, shook his head. 'But, Doc, something tells me that the rest of my life ain't gonna *be* so long if I don't even try.' He shrugged, staring out to sea. 'Time'll tell . . . and just look at what's coming in over the horizon. Beats the hell out of Santa and his sleigh.'

'What?' Adam looked, and his head spun to see a tall-masted ship approaching over the horizon. 'The *Pahalu*,' he breathed. 'Dad . . .' He looked between Stone and Chen, grinning uncontrollably. 'My dad's coming!'

Even Harm managed a smile, down on the sand. 'Hey,' she said croakily. 'Happy holidays.'

24: Start Ending

Adam watched and waited at the water's edge as the crowded life-raft washed in closer. *Most thirteen-year-old boys wait for their dads to get home from work in the evening*, he reflected, shaking his head. *Me . . .*

'Hey! Adam!'

Adam's battered heart very nearly gave out all together at the sound of the voice. He opened his mouth to call back, but the words dried in his throat as a tall, gawky figure stood up in the middle of the boat. He waved madly and Adam waved back as his father jumped in the water with an ungainly splash, almost lost his spectacles, swam and then waded through the water towards shore. Adam ran into the surf and into his dad's arms. He almost passed out from the pain of his crushed bruises, but hugged him right back. He found he couldn't let go, couldn't even look up into his dad's face, in case he was imagining things. Adam had figured he'd have so much to say at this moment, but right now words made way for tears.

That was OK.

He knew the feeling wouldn't last, but everything was OK right now.

An hour later, Adam stood at the cliff edge, a light breeze stirring the rags of his T-shirt, looking down at the graceful lines of the *Pahalu* dominating the inlet below. Wide black shadows washed beneath the idle surface of the glistening sea – the guardians of the shattered base. With their final task completed, their own systems had shut down.

'I can't believe what you've been through. I felt for sure I'd really lost you this time.'

Adam turned to his dad, sitting behind him on the turf, and nodded distantly. 'I guess things worked out in the end.' The wind rustled the undergrowth, and he found himself looking all around for any sign of raptors – a slither of scaly movement, the flash of an amber eye or the twitch of a claw. *They're gone now*, he told himself. *End of.*

Bill Adlar got slowly to his feet and stood beside Adam. 'I know I can't wave any wands to fix this. But now that the whole thing's over and we're back together . . .'

'It's not over, Dad.' Adam turned to him. 'I mean, OK, *here* it's over. The raptors are dead, but Samantha Josephs . . .' He hugged himself. 'She said she'd be back and it would be like the last three months never happened. She seemed to really believe it, but how——?'

Mr Adlar shrugged. 'She was badly injured. In shock. She's out of our lives now.' He put a hand on his son's back. 'And this time we have real evidence of what Geneflow has been doing. The sea monsters . . . the submarine Josephs used to get in and out . . . the bodies of the raptors . . . Chen's already interrogating one of their guards, I believe. You and I can go home now, Ad.'

'Now Doc Stone has patched him up properly, I guess,' said Adam.

'Helping the survivors seems to be keeping him busy.' Mr Adlar smiled. 'And making him happy too, I think. All told there'll be plenty to present to Doctor Marrs as evidence when he sends his UN peacekeeping force here to collect us in style . . .'

Adam forced a smile. 'A bit late as Christmas presents go. But I can deal with that.'

'He's already talking to the governors of the prisons who let their convicts be brought here,' said Mr Adlar. 'We'll have no end of leads to follow up.'

'Then you think we really might stop Geneflow?' Adam murmured. 'Whatever it is they're trying to do . . .'

'And we *might* really get to go back home!' Harm declared, walking out of the jungle, using a branch for a walking stick. 'Just imagine – TV. Music. Three meals a day. Sleeping in a bed.' She laughed suddenly. 'A bed! I mean, *what*? Are you serious?'

Adam grinned. 'Will you go back to your mum?'

'Maybe.' Harm shrugged. 'I was just drifting before, you know? Came out here wanting to meet up with my dad again, wanting something big to change my life.'

'You got that all right.'

'But I wanted it to change without me doing anything myself,' Harm said. 'The *new* me is never going to wait around for stuff to happen again.' She looked at Mr Adlar and smiled. 'So, while he's glad to see you and all, can you give us five minutes alone?'

Adam's dad raised his eyebrows and pretended to consider. 'I guess I can. Seeing as it's Christmas.' He winked at Adam and walked off into the jungle foliage. 'I'll catch you later.'

'You know it,' Adam said. He turned to Harm, curious. 'What's up?'

She looked at him. 'What did Alta-Vita mean again?'

'Er . . .' Adam cast his mind back. 'Life at its summit, or something.'

'I think David just reached his. I caught him and Lisa in camp. You know, she's busy feeding everyone out of that storeroom 'cause that's how she is, and he's helping her to do it 'cause that's how *he* is. And then, you know what she does?' She leaned forward and kissed Adam lightly on the lips. 'She does that.'

Startled, Adam felt his cheeks burn red. 'She, uh . . . she does?'

'I guess now they can get a room, they've gotten a room, right?' Harm smiled at him. 'See what a good new person I am? You nearly get me killed, and do I kick your butt? No, I limp all the way out here to kiss you just 'cause the sun is shining and life is sweet.' She looked out to sea. 'Or at least, it could be. Guess it's all down to me and my dreams, isn't it?'

Adam nodded. *Or someone else's nightmares*, he thought darkly. The ghost of Loner had caught in his thoughts, and Josephs' dying words seemed to carry on the breeze: '*The work will go on . . . You haven't even won breathing space.*'

But then he closed his eyes and tried to push away the fear and the violence that had haunted these last days. Christmas was meant to be a time for family, and for peace. Well, he'd found a kind of family here on Raptor Island. And for a time at least, in the sunshine and the stillness before Marrs arrived, maybe they could enjoy some peace together.

Adam stayed looking out with Harm from the summit. The sky stretched wide all around them, a pale and perfect blue. There wasn't a cloud on the horizon.

Not yet.

COMING SOON . . .

Prehistoric beasts merge with
nightmare visions of the future
as Geneflow's plans for the Earth
reach their final phase.

Reunited with the savage,
unpredictable Zed, Adam and some
unlikely allies must battle to stop the
evil scientists and their killer creations
before the ultimate apocalypse
is unleashed upon humanity . . .

Z.APOCALYPSE

**Don't miss Adam's first terrifying meeting
with Geneflow . . .**

YOU'RE A THIRTEEN-OLD-BOY ON THE RUN.

A MASSIVE, MAN-EATING DINOSAUR IS AFTER YOU.

EVIL SCIENTISTS WANT YOU BOTH DEAD

THERE'S ONLY ONE WAY OUT.

YOU AND THE MONSTER HAVE TO WORK TOGETHER . . .

Z.REX

by Steve Cole

'A terrific thriller that . . .
fans of Anthony Horowitz will love'
The Times

OUT NOW!

ISBN: 978 1 862 30777 3

If you enjoyed Z.RAPTOR, you'll love Steve Cole
and Chris Hunter's explosive series,

Read on for an extract from book one . . .

DAY ZERO – THE MOST HORRIFIC ATTACK
IN HISTORY – HAS CHANGED THE WORLD FOR EVER.

THE RULEBOOK'S JUST BEEN RE-WRITTEN.

Felix Smith is a soldier, a spy and
an expert in covert bomb disposal.

He's also a fifteen-year-old boy intent on
taking the fight straight to the terrorists.

The countdown is on.

NOT SUITABLE FOR YOUNGER READERS

ISBN: 978 0 552 56083 2

COUNTDOWN COMMENCING:
... TWENTY-SEVEN ...

Got you.

The sight of the bomb hit Felix like a punch in the guts.

Just twelve minutes remaining on the clock.

Wisps of CS gas hung in the air like ghostly fingers as he inched his way closer. Felix could hear the assault teams clearing the final few rooms around him – bursts of automatic gunfire and the rhythmic thud of the distraction grenades. He tried to tune out the swearing, the shouting, the commands barked out over loudhailers, and focus on staying calm. On doing his job.

The bomb looked ordinary. It could've been an oversized toolbox. Padlocked, of course. There was a digital LED clock on the outside. The numerals shone like laser sights, clustering on his brain.

Felix suddenly realized the building had become eerily

silent, as though the whole place was holding its breath. He could smell his own sweat and the two eyepieces on his S10 were starting to steam up. Again he willed himself to stay calm. A device of this size could wipe out the building and everyone in it in an instant. He was going to have to move fast.

There seemed to be no hidden devices on or around the bomb itself. He unfastened the zip on his assault vest and removed the XPAK explosives detector. He gave its baton a quick swipe over the case.

Pentanex 8, he realized. *Three times more powerful than TNT. If it detonates now we'll be vaporized.* Images crowded into his head as he imagined the outcome of a bomb like this one detonating. *A storm of debris smashing through the surrounding skyscrapers, pounding the vehicles below to scrap. Shards of glass slicing the air. Bodies charred to ash by the high-energy fireball . . .*

There were only ten minutes left on the clock now. Felix felt his body start to shake. *Get it together*, he told himself. *Got to breathe . . . got to focus . . .*

Everything's riding on this.

He took out his hand-entry kit from his bergen – his trusty backpack – and removed two picks. Carefully he worked them into the padlock. As he held the lock's spring-loaded teeth in place with the first pick, he took the pressure of the drum with the other and gave it a sharp clockwise tug. In seconds the padlock was free and the lid of the case was now a little looser – just enough to see if anything had been secreted around the lid. The sweaty seconds went on blinking away. Felix gingerly felt his way along the seal of the case for hidden switches, and as he got to the fourth side he could see the tiny silver bail arm of a micro-switch next to a light sensor.

Felix swore. The bomb was booby-trapped. He was going to have to cut in.

Quickly, precisely, he took out his gas-powered hot-knife – a small pen-like device with a sharp blade heated by a tiny gas cartridge – and made the first incision into the case. Seconds later he cut another, and another, until finally he had a small square hole just big enough to poke his night-vision monocular into.

Inside he could see the bomb's TPU, its timing and power unit: a small circuit board covered in electronic components, complete with detonators, a battery pack and the Pentanex 8, of course – there were maybe 50 kilos of the stuff.

His saliva was like thick paste as he swallowed hard. If he messed up now . . .

Go for the battery pack. Felix could hear his instructor's voice in his mind. *The TPU is the brain of the bomb, but the power source is its heart. Rip it out.*

Seven minutes left . . .

Cutting frantically away with the hot-knife, Felix felt alive, intoxicated with the rush of adrenaline. But there was dread there too, a sick feeling in his stomach. He knew he needed to extend the size of the hole first if he was to stand any chance of tracing the wires to the micro-switch. The noise of the assault teams had died. The only sound he could hear now was the thunder of his heart. Sweat made his black jumpsuit cling clammily to his skin.

Five minutes . . .

'Done it,' he breathed, aware of the sweat pooling at the bottom of his respirator. It wasn't perfect, but the hole was now big enough for Felix to have a dig around. He pushed his night-vision device further into the cavity, looking left and then right, and finally running under one of the packets of Pentanex. He held his breath. There were the two wires leading from the microswitch to the TPU.

We're in business. Felix pulled out a pair of surgical forceps, gripped the first of the wires and attached a probe to its plastic sheath. As he felt it bite into the shiny silver wire inside, something seemed to click inside him. Emotions bled away as almost mechanical action took over. His hands stayed steady as he grasped the second wire and did the same, his focus unfalteringly on the job in hand.

Four minutes . . .

He attached the handheld circuit detector and anxiously waited as it eworked its magic on the microswitch wires. For a moment he felt a surge of panic. *There's no time*, he thought, *no time for this*. But though he was right up against it, he knew he had to do this the right way.

Cut corners and you cut your own throat.

Felix clocked the reading on the circuit detector. The micro-switch was definitely a trigger. He knew that if he opened the lid he'd be blown to pieces. Already he was deftly removing the two probes so he could get to work on the micro-switch before removing it from the circuit.

Two minutes . . .

Not before time. Now, with the micro-switch out of the equation, he could open the lid and get to the TPU. Felix flicked open the two latches of the pelican case. Blood whammed through his temples as slowly, so slowly, he raised the lid . . .

Nothing

Now, get it cracked. Your whole life depends on it.

Felix knew that ideally he should remove the battery first. But it was partially obscured by the explosives, and with so little time left it made more sense to separate the explosives from the device instead. He got to work, meticulously cutting away chunks of Pentanex with his ceramic clasp-knife.

One minute remaining . . .

There were still about ten kilos of Pentanex left in the bomb – enough to blow him to smithereens – but Felix could see the whole circuit now. It was a standard timer circuit. He allowed himself a smile. He was safe to cut out the battery. Felix pulled his 'snips' – his wire-cutters – from his assault vest and leaned in to position the jaws either side of the battery's two connecting cables. He could almost feel the crisp clunk as they cut the thick-wound strands, his favourite sensation. *This one's in the bag! The bomb is dead . . .*

He allowed himself a look of satisfaction. *Finished.*

But some sudden instinct made Felix open his eyes.

To find the timer flashing down to zero.

He cried out, nothing coherent, rage and helplessness crushing in as a blinding white light swamped his eyes.

The sound of a blast shook through the room. Felix ripped off his respirator and goggles, shielded his eyes from the sudden burst of floodlights above him and watched a banner unfurl from the ceiling.

BOOM! You have just failed.